mai tais & mistletoe

katrina marie

prologue

"YES!" I throw my hands up. My nephew absolutely killed it on the field. The homecoming game for the peewee football team is in the books, and the team is undefeated.

My entire family is here, and we wait for the field to clear before we make our way down the bleachers. Even my nephew's sperm donor showed up to watch him play. At least he doesn't seem to start crap with my sister's boyfriend this time.

David, my nephew, is a natural when it comes to throwing the football around. Thanks to me, he's now one of the best in the peewee circuit.

He makes his way over to the stands, and I intercept him before he can get to my sister. "You did amazing out there, buddy."

"Thanks, Uncle Bryce." He wraps his arms around my waist and gives me a hug. His padding digs into me and I pull away. "Are you home to stay for a while?"

"Almost." Bending down, I look into his eyes. "But soon. I have to go back to finish out my schoolwork. Then I'll be home for good."

"Sweet," he lifts his hand for a high five, "will you practice with me some more? Carlos is cool, but his aim sucks."

"You bet." I'm glad he has Carlos now.

His dad has been in and out of his life since he was a baby. My brother and I have done the best we can to help Caroline with him, but it's not something we have been great at. I was still in junior high when she had him. He was always like a bonus sibling until I got older. There are just some things my sister doesn't understand, especially with sports.

"I'm gonna go find Mom."

"Alright, I'll meet you over there in a bit."

He rushes off to the group that has formed at the bottom row of the bleachers. Considering my sister has raised him on her own, with occasional help from us, I think he's turning out to be an amazing human. Proof you don't need two parents to have a happy childhood. Hell, I didn't, and I think I'm pretty fucking awesome.

"If he sticks with it, he's going to be an amazing addition to the high school football team." Coach King moves next to me on the sidewalk.

"He will. I've been coming home on the weekends to work with him on throwing."

"You're doing a good job," he pauses for a second, "if you hadn't stopped playing in college, you'd be a top pick for the draft."

Just like that, the high praise from my former coach is ruined. He really should learn how to talk to people. It's not like I quit the team for shits and giggles. My family needed me. My sister needed me, and I won't walk away from family.

"Well, because of that, I'll be done with my degree in a month." I stare at the field. Anything from asking him this question to his face. "I was actually wondering if you're hiring any coaching staff. I have no problem working my way up the ladder."

"You'll have to get with the administration. I know the high school staffing is full, but the junior high might be hiring."

"There's no room anywhere?"

"Sorry, son." He moves toward the fence and leans on the top. I'm not sure if I'm supposed to follow, or not, but I do. I need to know if there's anything I can do. "Do you have all the requirements?"

I don't know. I never thought about coaching until I started working with David. "I'll have my bachelors in physical education at the end of the year."

"That's not enough."

"Oh."

"What were you planning on using your degree for?"

That's a good question. One I hadn't considered because I have no idea. "I'm not sure. I figured I would look for a job as soon as I got my degree."

"In order for you to coach in school, you'll need to have your teaching certificate." Add that to the list of things I didn't know. It makes sense, though.

"Okay. How long does that take?"

"It should only take a year since you already have a degree. But get with admin. I know you want a spot on the high school coaching staff, but starting at the junior high isn't so bad."

He's right, but I don't even know if I like kids that age range. David isn't quite there yet, and I don't know anyone with kids that age. "I'll think about it."

"If you decide to go some other route, let me know and I'll give you a recommendation. You were one of my best athletes. These kids could learn a thing or two from you."

"Thanks." He walks off, leaving me to my thoughts. He's given me a lot to think about, but I don't know if it's something I truly want to do. Not when I'm so close to being done with school. It could be worth it.

"Uncle Bryce!" David calls and I turn around to see him waving me over, "we're going to eat. You should come with us."

"I'll meet you there."

"Okay," he glances over at Caroline and scrunches his nose, "Mom says I have to go home and take a shower first, though."

"It's a good idea," I act like I'm smelling him, "you stink."

"I guess." He frowns before following them to the parking lot.

Mom stands beside me and puts her arm around my shoulder. "It'll be nice having you home for good next month. The house is lonely with all you kids moving out and living your own adventures."

"Yep." I don't plan on staying there long, but I'm not going to ruin her mood tonight. "It'll be nice to have home-cooked meals again."

"Good to know," she pulls her arm away, "what did Coach want?"

"To talk about David. He's already got his eye on him."

"I figured as much. You were over there for quite a while to only be talking about him."

I could tell her about the rest of the conversation, but not yet. Not until I know what I want to do. The hard part is almost over, and I feel like I'm a freshman again, trying to figure out what I want to be when I grow up. "It wasn't anything."

"Hmm." She knows there was more, but she isn't going to pressure me about it. "Are you riding to the restaurant with me?"

"No, I'll meet you there."

"Okay. Be careful."

I watch her walk away, and can't help but wonder how my life would have turned out had my dad decided to stay. Nothing I can do about that now. I pull my keys out of my pocket, and head toward my car. There's enough time for me to hit up Out of the Ashes before we eat.

1

bryce

HOME AT LAST. Well, not home. I'm at the bar with my sister. It's her weekly girl's night, and I asked if I could tag along.

I need to get out of the house already and I was only there long enough to put my boxes and bags in my room. Mom was trying to force feed me her food. It's not that it's bad, but damn...let me get settled in.

"So, what are you going to do now?" Kate, one of my sister's friends, asks. I don't miss the way she leans over and shows her cleavage. Or the glare Caroline is shooting her from the other side of the table.

"I'm not sure. I'm still working through some things." I look everywhere but in her direction. While she might be trying to get my attention, I think she forgets I've known her my entire life. She's like a bonus annoying sister, and been nothing more than that. Reaf, on the other hand, had a crush on her when we were younger.

"Well, if you need a job in the meantime, we could always use some muscle at the flower shop."

"I think we're good, Kate." My sister grins, but her tone is a whole different vibe. A warning to her friend to knock it off.

"No offense, but I'm good." There's no way in hell I'd work with my sister all day. I love her to death, but no. "I actually thought about seeing if they need help here during the holidays. At least, until I figure things out."

"I can talk to Carlos. I know they are doing a grand opening of the stage area this month."

"I'm a big boy, Care. I can apply for the job myself."

"Okay, okay," she raises her hands in surrender, "I was just trying to help."

Damn. I've hurt my sister's feelings now. "I'm going to get another drink. Anybody need a refill?"

Everyone raises their hand, and I make a mental note of what they're drinking. I weave around the crowd to the bar. Carlos is at one end of the bar with customers gathered around him. There's another bartender at the end and he seems less busy.

Someone moves out of the way, and I take their spot. "How can I help you?"

There's time for a quick glance at his name tag. "Hi, Eric, I need two beers, and..." My mind goes blank at the names of their drinks.

"You're Caroline's brother, right?"

Is it that obvious? "Yes. I'm here with her and her friends."

"No worries on remembering their drinks. I know what they like." Thank God because there's no way in hell I was remembering all the cocktails. At least my sister is easy. She drinks the same thing I do.

"Thanks, man." I lean against the bar and wait while he pours the drinks. "Any chance you're hiring?"

"I'm not sure." He shakes a drink in a metal canister. "I'm

mostly in charge of the bar, but I can ask Angie when she comes in tomorrow."

"That's okay. I'll stop by then." I glance at all the drinks he's set in front of me and wonder how I'm going to get them to the table.

"Do you want me to get someone to help you with that?" Eric nods at the cluster of drinks.

"It might take me two trips, but I think I can handle it."

Eric laughs, but before I can even grab one of the drinks a hand grabs one of the drinks. "Here, I'll help you."

"Aren't you supposed to be taking care of the guests, Delilah?" Eric lifts an eyebrow.

Time to see who my rescuer is. I turn and see the most beautiful girl I've ever seen. Straight brown hair falls just past her shoulders, and her eyes are wide when she sees me. She looks familiar, but I can't quite place where I've seen her outside of the bar. I mean, I've noticed her, but haven't paid too much attention.

"As you can see, Eric, there's not a line." He doesn't say anything and moves onto his next customer.

"Thanks. You don't have to help me if you have a job to do." I put my hand through the handle of two of the mugs and try to figure out how I'm going to grab the other two glasses, plus the one she's holding.

"It's okay, Bryce. It's not a big deal."

"Ok—" wait a minute, "how do you know my name?"

She looks down at the ground before meeting my eyes. "Why wouldn't I?" she scoffs. "We went to the same school. Hell, we graduated in the same class."

That's not possible. Asheville High isn't very big. I could have sworn I knew everyone in my grade. "There's no way."

"There is." She grabs one of the cocktails. "We didn't exactly run in the same circles. You had your team, and I had my small group of friends."

"And who were they?"

"Nobody you would know." She walks toward the table my sister and her friends are standing around. I have no choice but to follow her.

My brain is in overdrive trying to puzzle through how I got through high school without knowing who she is.

"You know we could have gotten someone on the waitstaff to bring our drink order, right?" My sister's other friend Samantha asks as Delilah and I approach the table.

"Oh," I set Emily's cocktail in front of her while Delilah hands the other two to Sam and Kate, "I actually didn't know that."

"It's something you'll have to learn if you plan on getting a job here." Caroline smiles as I pass her one of the mugs of beer.

"True." I turn to tell Delilah thank you for the help, but she's already gone. Her back faces us as she stands at the host podium.

"So, who is everyone bringing to the grand opening of the stage area?" Kate takes a sip of her drink. "I could always use a date, Bryce."

She whimpers at the same time a thud hits the table. If I had to guess, my sister kicked her. "I'm not making any plans until I know if I have a job or not."

"Smart thinking, little brother," Caroline bumps into me, "though, there's technically two grand openings. One for employees and their partners, and one for the public."

"Looks like I'm picking a good time to apply." I grin at my sister. My gaze moves back toward the front of the bar and lands on Delilah's eyes before she turns her focus. "Hey, Care, does Mom still have my old yearbooks?"

2

delilah

"ARE YOU OKAY?" Eric asks as I make my way toward the front of the bar.

"Yeah, fine."

I shouldn't be surprised Bryce doesn't know who I am. I didn't hang out with the popular kids. Not like my twin did, anyway. Though, I'm sure he will remember him by name alone. He was always running around with the jocks while I was sitting at home with my romcom movies and popcorn, always feeling like an outsider.

"Are you sure? You don't look like it." He's not letting this go. I don't know why he feels like he has to get involved in everyone's love life, or lack thereof. He acts like an overprotective parent, but we're the same age. Or close to it, anyway.

"Yep." I walk past the bar and take up my station at the stand in front of the door. Maybe we won't be busy for the rest of the night and I can go home to decompress. Little does Bryce know I had a crush on him way back when, and him not even knowing who I am? That was a punch in the gut.

A small group of people walk through the door. Loud and obnoxious as they approach me.

"We need a table for six." One of them demands as they walk in. So much for my easy night.

"Let me see what we have open." I leave my stand to check the sitting area. Bryce's attention is on me, and I don't know how I feel about that. The second our gazes meet, I look away. Why did I have to help him out tonight after avoiding him every other time he's come in?

The only table big enough to seat this group is occupied. It looks like they are finishing up. I keep my eyes on the floor as I make my way back to my stand. "It's going to be about a fifteen-minute wait."

"Y'all seriously only have one table big enough to fit us?" I've never seen this guy, or any of his group, in here before so he may not know we're mostly a bar.

As much as I want to pop off, I need to keep my cool. Making rent on my own since Lisa went off on her grand adventure has been tough. "Yes, we have plenty of high-top tables if you don't mind being separated."

He leans closer, his upper body hovering over the stand, and I instinctively take a step back. "If we wanted to sit away from each other, I wouldn't have asked for a table to seat us all."

I feel someone behind me. "Look, man, she's just doing her job. There's no need to be an asshole."

"And who the hell are you?" This time the man steps around the stand and is standing directly in front of me.

Bryce moves in front of me, putting me out of harm's way. "I'm just here to have a few drinks. But couldn't help but over-hear the way you were speaking to Delilah. That's not some-thing I can stand by."

Oh, dear God. Why is he doing this? He told me not

twenty minutes ago he doesn't even remember who I am. There's no reason for him to be here defending my honor.

"We can take this outside," the patron says and takes another step toward Bryce.

Eric comes rushing up. "That won't be necessary, Sir," he puts himself between Bryce and the man being a jerk, "you can wait patiently for the table you requested, or you can go to one of the other fine establishments in Asheville."

The guy looks at each of us, his hands clenched into fists. A part of me thinks this guy came in here looking for trouble. I wait, wondering which route this guy is going to go. I hate when we get customers like him, though it doesn't happen often.

Finally, he releases his hands and takes a step back. "Come on, let's find somewhere else to eat. This place looks like a dump, anyway."

A sigh escapes me as soon as they are out the door. Bryce turns to me, "Are you okay?"

I nod. It's the only thing I can do. While I'd like to say those guys would have chilled out had Bryce not come over here, I don't know if they would have. I've never had someone lean into my space like that. I'm a zero-conflict type of person, and that is way outside of my comfort zone.

Eric taps Bryce on the shoulder, pulling his attention away from me. "Thanks for stepping in for Delilah, but you can't do that. It could have ended badly for the bar."

"Sorry, I was just trying to help."

"I know, dude. But I had an eye on the situation," he points to the bar, and some of my coworkers are in this corner instead of where they usually are, "so did they."

"I'll, uh, remember that," he looks down at me and smiles, "I'm glad you're okay."

"Thanks."

Eric and I watch him go back to the table. "Want to tell me what that was about?"

"I honestly have no clue. We went to school together, but he didn't know I existed."

"Well," he bumps into my shoulder, "he knows you do now."

"Obviously," I roll my eyes and move toward the podium, "at least he doesn't come in here often."

"For now." Eric laughs and heads back toward his station at the bar.

What did he mean by that? I know he graduated recently, but that doesn't mean he's going to stick around Asheville. He was talking to Eric about something when I walked up earlier, but I didn't think to ask what it was about. It's not really my business.

If there's one thing I've learned living in this town, it's to keep your head down and focus on yourself. If not, you'll be the talk of the town without meaning to be.

Caroline and her friends leave after another hour. Since her and Carlos started dating, he's taken off more during the week. He knows how important her girl's night is, and helps out with her son while she has a few drinks with her friends.

Bryce? He doesn't leave, though. He stops by the bar again, talking to Eric. Now my curiosity is peaked. I need to know what they're discussing. I'll ambush Eric while closing up.

After a few minutes, Bryce walks past the podium I'm standing behind and heads for the door. Before he opens it, he turns toward me. "See you later, Delilah."

I wave because all common sense has left my body and my mouth can't form words. He pushes the door open and a blast of cold air hits me. What did he mean by see you later?

3

bryce

MOM'S CAR isn't in the driveway when I pull in. Where the hell is she? Carlos is taking care of David, so she's not at my sister's house. The only thing I can think of is she had a date. Or, maybe she went to eat with friends. Either way, it's inconvenient.

I guess I'll have to find the yearbooks on my own. A gust of wind pushes the door open wider than I expect when I get out of the car, and I pull the hood of my jacket up to keep my ears from getting cold on the way to the door. It's definitely colder than it was when I left the bar. I'm not a fan. It's why I went to school in south Texas. It's warmer there, and I don't have to worry about this nonsense as much.

My fingers tremble as I press the code into the keypad to unlock the door. As soon as I open the door, I rush inside and close the door behind me. Fuck the cold. I turn on the light in the living room and pull my jacket off, throwing it on the couch.

I'm not sure where Mom has all the stuff from when my

siblings and I graduated, but the first place I'm looking is the hall closet. Opening the door, I stare at the stacks of boxes on the floor. My gaze travels up and there's even more on the rack above. How much crap does she keep stored in here?

The hall light sucks and I grab the first box and set it on the living room floor before grabbing a few more. Should I have started with one? Probably. But, if it's not in there I have more boxes in my area to look through. The wood floor is cold when I sit down, and I pull the throw blanket off the couch to push under me. Let's do this.

The cardboard tears as I pull open the flaps of the first box. Damn it. Hopefully tape will fix it. Halloween decorations are nestled in the confines. I doubt the yearbooks will be in here, but I better make sure. Something pokes my finger as I rummage through the box, and a bead of blood forms on my fingertip. This is definitely not my night.

"What are you doing?"

"Shit." Twisting toward the door, I see Mom staring at me as if I've lost my mind. "You scared me."

"Sorry. I wasn't quiet when I opened the door." She closes the door behind her and peels her coat off before hanging it on the rack. She glances at the jacket I threw on the couch and does the same with it. "What are you doing, though?"

"Um, you know the girl that works the door at the bar?"

"Delilah? Yes, I know her. But what does she have to do with this?" She waves her hand over the mess I've made in the living room.

"We bumped into each other tonight and she swears we went to school together." I point into the box in front of me. Which clearly does not hold the yearbooks. "And I wanted to see if she actually did."

"You were in the same graduating class, Bryce." Mom shakes he head, and grabs one of the boxes, putting it back in the closet. I don't miss her disappointed tone. She points at my finger, "You should get a band-aid for that."

"I'm fine," I shake my head, "how do you know?"

"I was at your graduation, son. She walked across the stage right after her brother."

"Who is her brother?" I think she mentioned him.

"Seriously?" Mom puts her hands on her hips and I know I'm about to get my ass chewed out despite being an adult. "Devin was here all the time. You played football together."

"I never realized he had a twin sister."

"Well, he did," she turns back toward the hall, "get these boxes put up before you go to bed, please."

The fact she doesn't want to discuss anything tells me I've fucked up. And I know I have. I feel like a douche for not noticing her back then. Now, though, she has my full attention. Shaking my head, I close the box and stand. And that right there makes me a dick, but I don't care. I need to know more about her. Hopefully, I get the job at the bar and I'll get to spend more time with her.

* * *

Delilah isn't at the bar when I open the door. Logically, I could work wherever I want until I figure out what I want to do with my degree. Especially after my coach told me I'd need to get certified to coach at the school.

Eric waves as I approach the bar, "so, you were serious about the job?"

"Yep," I tap on the counter, "at least for a bit. Is Angie here today? If not, I can talk to whoever can hire me."

I hope like hell it's Angie. If not, I'm not so sure I'd like the outcome. "Why do you need a job?"

Fuck. That's what I was afraid of. I turn toward Carlos. "Because I'm currently unemployed." He's with my sister most of the time. Surely, he knows that. "I just need an income until I decide what my next step is."

"That makes sense." He crosses his arms over his chest and nods. "Do you have any idea what you want to do?"

He's trying to pull off this whole fatherly act, and frankly...I'm not a fan. If I need advice, I'll go to one of my siblings or my mom. I don't need him putting his nose where it doesn't belong. For now, though, I'll play nice. His relationship with my sister is still relatively new, and I don't want to put a wedge between them. She's finally happy, and I won't be the person who ruins what she deserves.

"Not yet. But I'm considering a few things."

"That's good." All of that for him to tell me that's good? I swear, sometimes I don't understand this guy. But whatever. I'm almost certain he's going to be a part of the family sooner than later.

"So, can I get a job here? I don't exactly want to be mooching off my mom until I figure shit out."

Carlos looks at me then Eric before focusing on me again. "Sure, I'm cool with it. I mean, you can't bartend, but you can help with the waitstaff and maybe even bouncer duties when we open up the stage area next weekend."

"Sounds good." There's hardly anyone here right now. "Um, when can I start?"

"I'll get you the paperwork." Carlos turns toward the hallway. "Fill it out, and bring it back. We'll get you started the next day. Angie needs time to add you into the system."

Eric leans against the bar and grins. "Welcome to the team. We're a fun bunch."

"Believe me, I know."

The door opens, and I turn to see who walked in. Delilah stops in her tracks.

4

delilah

WHY IS HE HERE? I thought I'd only have to see him at night, when he usually comes in. Not during the day. It's bad enough I do my best to ignore him any other night he's stopped by. Last night shouldn't have been different, but I couldn't watch him struggle with the drinks.

Eric notices me at the same time. "Morning. Bryce will be working with us soon."

My mouth drops open. What the hell? Bryce turns his head to the side in confusion, and I snap my jaw closed. I don't want to seem rude. Even though I want to demand answers. Want to know why he's suddenly interested in a job here. Especially after realizing I went to school with him. It seems fishy.

"Oh." What do they want me to say? Up until last night, he didn't know I existed.

"That's all you have to say, Del? We're getting more help when we'll need it most." Eric is watching my every move. After last night, I'm sure he's already trying to figure out a way to play matchmaker. He's just as bad as the rest of the people here. I'm perfectly happy being single. Especially when the person in question is Bryce.

"Welcome to the team?" My voice raises at the end and I shrug. "I'm gonna clock in and get ready for the day."

Bryce is the obstacle between me and the office. He's standing in the middle of walkway. I could go around through the tables and come out the other side, but it'd be obvious I'm avoiding him. That would be rude. Taking a deep breath, I gather my courage and head in his direction. There isn't much space to get by him, and I turn to the side to give myself more space. Only I turn the wrong way, and my hand brushes against his.

The slight touch is enough to send a zing through my arm and it pisses me off. I rush toward the office to keep from embarrassing myself.

I lusted after him when I was in high school. He was the star quarterback, and I was the reserved girl who stuck to herself. I will not go down that path again.

Not much has changed since then, either. We're both the same as we were back then. Now, though, I'm older and I know better. That road leads to long nights wondering what I can do to get his attention knowing damn well nothing will come of it. I can't be that person again. Even if he seems to have finally noticed me. Well, too late buddy. I'm older, wiser, and know myself better, now.

Stomping into the office, I toss my bag on an empty shelf. Him working here could pose a problem, and I really want to know if his reasons for wanting a job is a coincidence or if I'm the reason.

"Woah, what's the matter with you?"

My heart leaps into my throat, or at least it feels like it does. "Crap. I didn't know you were in here, Carlos."

"Obviously," he has a stack of papers in his hands, and I know they are for Bryce, "so, what's the problem?"

Do I tell him? I mean, he's always been an amazing boss. Though, I'm not sure how well he handles issues with employees, and I really don't want to admit the sting I felt yesterday when Bryce didn't know who I was.

"Nothing, just a rough start to the morning." That's an understatement, but it's the only explanation he's getting. For now, at least. If Bryce becomes a problem, I'll have to talk to Carlos about shift changes. Which I'll hate to do because I know they need me more in the evenings when the tables are full.

Ugh. He's yet again, four years later, making me question what I should do. Deep breaths, Delilah. You can work with him and not give him brain space.

"Okay," he draws out the word, "I'll be around if you need to get things off your chest."

Forcing a smile, I take a seat on one of the chairs. "Thanks. I'll be out there to set up the tables for lunch in a moment."

Fake it 'til you make it will be my motto for the foreseeable future. I don't want Angie, Carlos, or Eric thinking I can't handle my job because of a fellow employee. I could find another one, but I love working here. Meeting new people and making sure they have a great experience are things that fill me with joy. Aside from the jerks who showed up last night and left after Bryce put them in their place.

Okay, so maybe having him step in wasn't so bad. It actually felt kind of nice. That was before I found out we'll be coworkers. Before I knew we were going to be in the same space. How am I going to keep those old crush feelings from coming up?

Nope. I'm not going down that road. I shake my head to physically, and mentally, push those thoughts away. It will be a busy morning getting the bar decorated for the holidays, and I don't have time to dwell on past emotions. It serves no purpose except to freak me out over something I can't control.

Enough wallowing, it's time to get to work. Pulling my hair together, I put it in a ponytail as I make my way out of the office into the bar area. To my surprise Bryce is no longer there. Carlos is making a list of things on a notepad and Eric is pulling chairs off the tables. Something he shouldn't even be doing because it's my job.

"You good, Del?" he asks as I pull a chair off a table.

"Yeah, I'm fine." It's a lie. I'm nowhere close to fine, but I'll manage.

I make my way around the tables, pulling down chairs and double checking the space between them. My focus is on my job, and I don't realize Eric has stopped helping and is now standing a few feet away from me.

He glances toward the bar area to make sure Carlos is occupied. "Are you sure? Is it because of Bryce? Is him working here going to be an issue for you?"

How is it this person who is barely older than me can zero in on my thought process without me saying a word? "No, it'll be fine."

"You can tell me to mind my own business," he crosses his arms over his chest, "but I feel like there's history between you."

Snorting, I shake my head. "More like a non-existent history. I crushed on him hard in high school, and he didn't know I was even there. My brother played on the football team with him. Do you know how shitty it feels to know Bryce was good friends with him, but didn't know he had a twin sister?"

"Ouch. That's pretty painful," he moves to pat my shoulder, but stops at the glare I shoot his way, "if it becomes a problem, I'll shift his schedule around yours. I know I was being a pain last night with pushing you together, but I'll stop.

I don't want to do anything that makes you feel uncomfortable."

"Thanks, Eric." Even though he can be annoying, he's wise beyond his years. I mean he saw the Carlos and Caroline thing before almost everyone else.

"When you're done, Carlos wants you to get with him about what decorations he needs to pick up."

"I can do that." It's another thing to keep my mind off Bryce and what having him in my space will do, and I'm glad for the busy work.

5

bryce

IT'S BEEN ages since I've filled out paperwork, and I don't even know if I have a pen I can reach in my stuff. Pulling the middle drawer out of my desk, I shuffle through the papers. At least my mom didn't turn my room into a guest room, or craft room, like she did with my brother and sister's. I think some part of her knew I'd be back after college. Though, I definitely don't intend on staying here.

No luck with a pen. The wheels of my chair get caught on the chair mat, and I almost fall backward before standing up. Surely, she has pens somewhere in the junk drawer. I head toward the kitchen, bypassing the fridge until I come to the corner of the counter. Please still be a junk drawer. I haven't had to look in here since high school.

The drawer creaks as I pull it open. She obviously hasn't been in here lately, either. I rummage around until I find a pen, but that's not what stops me. An envelope with my mom's name on it peeks out on the side, and it doesn't look like my sister's writing. I grab it and pull out the contents. It's a small card and graduation picture.

Opening the card, I read the words, "Thank you for the notebooks and headband," the bottom is signed Delilah. I take a closer look at the picture included, and it's Devin standing next to who I'm now realizing is Delilah. They don't look alike. Well, not much. Where his face is angular, hers is round and softer. A lot different than how she looks now. Though, now she really does look more like her brother, and I'm not sure how I didn't realize that before.

That explains the look she gave earlier when she saw me at the bar. I vaguely remember her, but I thought she was younger than Devin. I didn't realize they were the same freaking age. Now I feel like a complete douche about our interaction last night. No wonder she didn't look thrilled I'd be working there.

"Bryce," my mom calls from the front of the house, "are you home?"

"Yeah, I'm in the kitchen." I shove the card and picture back into the envelope, and toss it in the drawer before slamming it shut.

"What are you doing?"

Act normal. Like you didn't just realize how much of an asshole you are, and figure out exactly who Delilah is. "Nothing. I needed a pen."

"For what?" She sets a bag on the table, and pulls out a few groceries.

I could have sworn I told her about applying for a job. "The application for Angie. I'm going to work at the bar until I figure out exactly what I want to do."

"Okay." She shrugs and puts up the food she just bought.

"What are you doing home? I thought you were at work." I need to move away from this drawer. It feels like my hovering by it is sending out a signal that I've done something I'm not supposed to. Technically, I did. That envelope wasn't meant for me, but I read the contents anyway.

"It's my lunch hour. I always get any last minute groceries at this time." As she's talking, I move from the counter as nonchalantly as possible. I don't want her to think I'm being weird. Though, that's probably exactly what I look like.

"Oh." I move around the island in the middle of the kitchen and take a seat at the table. It's bigger than anything we need on a daily basis, but she keeps it this way so we all have a place to sit when my siblings and their families come over. "Do you want me to make you anything for lunch?"

"No, I'm fine." She waves me away before sitting at a chair across from me. "I ate on the way over here. It's nice having you home, even if it's only until you get on your feet." She nods toward the pen I'm holding in my hand. "When do you start working? Do you have a plan for how long it'll be?"

This is the part where she grills me about all my plans. I don't blame her, but I'm not a teenager anymore. I'll figure life out. Maybe. "As soon as I take the application to Angie. Once she has me in her system, I'll start working."

"What are you thinking about doing after that?"

This is the part I'm unsure of. "I might go back to school again."

"But you just got out."

"I know. But...if I want to coach at one of the schools, I need a teaching certificate. And for that, I have to go back to school."

"You can do other things."

She's not wrong. While my degree is pretty limited for the most part, there are other things I can do. I just don't know if I want to do them since almost all of them require to be around adults. "I know. I'm weighing my options. I want to make sure I can afford to take care of myself, but I also want to do something I love. Why settle on a career I despise."

She nods and a small, smile forms on her lips. "You are absolutely right. And don't worry about finances. I'll help you out as long as you need it. There's no need to stress about it."

"Thanks." She means it, too. Little does she know I'm not going to take advantage of her kindness. I fully intend to pay rent while I'm here and help out with everything else. Like I said, I'm not a teenager anymore. Besides how can I show Delilah I've changed from that boy I was in high school who thought he was a big shot.

"I'm going to head back to work," she pats my hand, "let me know if you need anything, and when you start working."

"Yes, ma'am," I stand when she gets up and walk her to the door, "stay warm, Mom. As soon as I'm done filling this out, I'm going to run it up to Angie."

"Good luck." She waves, and I watch her as she heads to her car. Gratitude fills my chest at the type of woman my mom is. She's thoughtful and caring. She sent a gift to someone I didn't interact with out of the kindness in her heart. Hopefully, I can show Delilah the apple doesn't fall too far from the tree.

6

delilah

WHEN CARLOS LEFT for the store, I didn't expect him to bring back multiple boxes for decoration. "This is too much. Where am I supposed to hang everything?"

"That is for you to figure out, Delilah. Or you can call Stella and ask," he shrugs and walks toward the bar, "this was all her idea to begin with."

He's not amused by all the extra things Stella wants us to do. Honestly, as the one who has to put it all up, I'm not either. But I get where she's coming from. We're a small town bar, and even though we're on the upscale side during the evenings, she wants those who come in for lunch to be cozy.

The lunch crowd is slow and I take a few tables in the back to sort through everything. I push aside one box, and stop in my tracks. "Wait. Why do we have a tree? I didn't put that on there."

"Call Stella," Carlos yells across the room. The few patrons we have laugh, and I know they get a kick out of it. That's the problem with small towns. Everyone knows everyone, and if there's any discourse you can bet the entire town knows about it before the end of the day. I can only imagine what people will say when they hear I was questioning a tree.

"Fine," I huff. I don't know where she even thinks it will go since we're already at capacity every night. Well, we won't be in the next week or so. We're going to kick off the grand opening of the additional building soon, and my brother will be performing. So, there will be room. But not until that happens.

Picking up my phone, I look for Stella's number and open her contact.

DELILAH

> Where do you want me to put the tree? Or any of these decorations? It's a lot.

"You rang."

The box shifts to the edge of the table when I bump into it at the sound of Stella's voice. "How did you get here so fast?"

"I was in the office with Angie going over the last minute preparations for the stage opening."

Shifting my feet, I peer around her shoulder to see what Carlos is doing. Both him and Eric have their hands over their mouths trying to cover their laughs. "You could have told me."

"This was way more fun." Eric answers for our boss. Of course, he would think that.

"Now that you've had your fun, bring me a ladder," Stella orders them and that shuts them up pretty fast. She's one of the sweetest people I've ever met, but when she's in project mode...all bets are off. She becomes very demanding. "The wreathes and mistletoe will be easier once they get back with the ladder. For now, I'll help you with the tree."

"Which is going where?" I glance around the room trying to find an open space.

"The front door, next to you."

"Does it have to?" She's already nodding before I finish my sentence. "Okay, I guess let's do this. I need to have most of this stuff up before the evening crowd comes in."

"What are we waiting for?" With that, we both grab the tree box and heft it toward the front of the bar.

* * *

Stella was right about the tree, though I'm not telling her that. The sun is going down and the way the lights shimmer on the tree through window is magical. She even had Carlos pick up ornaments that resonate with each of us, which is pretty cool.

There are only a few more things I need to hang up before the night crowd rolls in. The fake mistletoe in hand, I climb up the ladder. I hope this is a good enough spot for Stella. She left a few hours ago and isn't here to direct me. But it makes sense here. It's the first doorway people go through when they sit down to eat, or grab a table to drink with their friends. I'm not sure where else I would put it that wouldn't require us buying another ladder to reach it. Sometimes I think Stella forgets I'm shorter than her, but also too hard-headed to ask for help.

Grabbing one of the hooks on the top of the ladder, I begin screwing it into the framing. I have to put all my strength into it, and wish I had a drill. I glance down to see if anyone has come in, but nobody is at the podium. With the hook in place, I pick up the mistletoe and loop the ribbon onto the hook. A few quick tugs is proof it won't move once I climb down the ladder.

A gust of wind follows the bell dinging over the door, and now I know someone is here. I don't bother looking down to confirm. "Give me just a moment and I'll be right with you."

Of course, someone would come in while I'm up here. I guess it's a good thing I didn't wear a dress. That could potentially be embarrassing. I take a step down, but in my rush, I miss the step. My arms windmill, fingers grasping in the air to find something to grab onto. Oh crap. This is going to hurt. I close my eyes and prepare for impact, and what's likely to be an expensive hospital visit.

My body never meets the floor. I fall into someone. Arms wrap around me. "Thanks Er— " The words die on my lips as I open my eyes and see who came to my rescue.

"Sorry to disappoint." Bryce grins down at me. His fingers are cold through my thin sweater. "It looked like you could use some help."

"Oh, um, thanks." He's closer to me than I ever imagined, and literally saved me. No. Don't go there. He's doing exactly what anyone else would have. I glance to the side. The few patrons we have are staring at me. Not one of them made a move to help. Eric is halfway around the bar. And the ladder? The stupid ladder is still standing right where I left it. Why couldn't it follow in my fall? If it did, I'd probably have it on top of me. So, maybe it's a good thing it didn't.

"Are you okay?" He's searching my face for any signs of pain.

I try to lift myself up, but he doesn't let me. Wanting a verbal answer before he'll let go. "I think so."

Finally, he releases me and helps me to my feet. "Are you sure?"

Nodding, I take a step and wince at the pain in my ankle. "Maybe not."

He calls over his shoulder, "Eric, can you get some ice over here?"

Eric doesn't hesitate. He turns to one of the other bartenders and gives the order. He grabs a chair from the closest table and pulls it toward me. "You really don't have to do all this."

"I know." He helps me sit down and lifts my leg. "May I?"

"Yes." He pushes my pants leg up and takes off my shoe. Two presses on my ankle and I wince in pain.

"It doesn't feel broken. We'll get some ice on it, and you'll have to stay off it the rest of the night."

"Really, I'll be fine." I'm still trying to figure out how he knows all this.

"You will be after you stay off your feet." Eric comes up behind him and hands him a small bag of ice. "Hold this there as long as you can. I'm going to talk to Angie. What were you doing up there anyway?"

"Hanging decorations." He looks up and sees which decoration it is, and I don't miss the sly smile play across his lips.

"Nice." I know he's thinking this is going to be an easy reason to kiss me, but I'm not going to play that game. He surprises me when he lifts my hand to his lips and places a small kiss on the back of it. "Stay here. I'll be back."

My face is warm and I know my cheeks are tinged red. My hand feels warm where his lips touched it, and I know right now. Working with him is definitely going to be a problem.

7

bryce

SHOULD I have kissed her hand? I'm not sure, but she didn't yank it away. It's a much better reaction to my presence than she had earlier today. Angie needs to know what happened, though. I'm pretty sure it isn't broken, but she does need to get it checked out.

I make my way toward the hallway. I've never been back here, but I know the office is in this direction. I pass the restrooms and come to a door at the very end. It's slightly ajar, and I knock on it a couple of times. It takes a few moments, but finally Angie calls, "Come in."

Pushing the door open I step inside. It doesn't look how I thought it would. It's very basic, and nothing like Stella has decorated in the actual bar. This feels more like the way it was when her uncle was alive. At least, from what I've been told. "Um, Angie."

"I was wondering when you'd be by. Did you get the application filled out?"

A quick glance at my empty hands makes me groan. "Yes,

but I left it on the podium up front. Delilah fell while hanging mistletoe."

"She what?" Angie stands and rushes around her desk.

"When I was coming in to turn in my application, I'm pretty sure she thought I was a customer. She said she'd be right with me and lost her footing hurrying down the ladder."

"Come on." Angie marches to the door and throws it wide open before hurrying down the hall. I'm assuming she wants me to follow and I rush to catch up. "Is she okay?"

"I think she only sprained her ankle, but she should probably get it checked out. It's pretty swollen."

Angie mumbles something under her breath along the lines of asking for help, but the music from the bar is so loud, I can't hear all of it. "Where is she?"

"I left her by the podium in a chair with a bag of ice." She's still there. One hand holding the ice to her ankle and the other pointing toward the tables. Eric is in front of the podium, and he looks lost.

She catches me and Angie walking toward her and rolls her eyes. "I see you tattled."

"It's not tattling. It's a work-related injury." Angie says with her hands on her hips. "Why didn't you ask for help?"

"Seriously?" She laughs and adjusts her posture. "When have I ever asked for help?"

Angie only shakes her head. "Well, you need to get it checked out."

"This is the foot I drive with. I'd have to try to get ahold of my brother and wait on him to get here."

I'm not sure what comes over me. Maybe the fact I want to get to know her better. Or, maybe it's because I was here when it happened and I want to make sure she's fine. "I can take her."

"No, I can wa—"

Angie cuts her off. "Done. Eric, you look like you're struggling up here. Send one of the bartenders over here, and I'll come up when it starts getting busy."

"Yes, ma'am." He runs to the bar like his life depends on it. Most likely from the daggers Delilah is shooting me with her eyes. I don't blame him.

"My car is right outside." I point as if she can see it through the door. "You have two options. I can carry you out, or let you lean on me for balance."

She stands and winces the second she puts weight on her foot. "I can walk out of here just fine." She starts toward the door, wincing with every step she takes.

"Keep an eye on her," Angie whispers to me.

"I will. Any particular doctor?"

"Take her to the urgent care downtown. They are great to work with."

I salute her. "You got it. Oh," I grab the papers off the podium, "here's my application."

"Thanks," Angie takes them from me and turns, "keep me updated."

I wave to Eric before following Delilah out of the bar. He's shaking his head, but I don't miss the smirk. Should I be worried?

* * *

"Are you okay back there?" I feel kind of bad for putting her in the back seat but it was the only place that makes sense. I pushed everything to one side, grabbed a few of the hoodies that were laying around that barrel, and use them to elevate her foot on top of the console.

"Yeah, I'm fine." She's not wrong I don't remember her being as snarky as she is now. I feel like if this was the way she was back then, I would definitely remember who she is. "How much longer until we get there? You're driving really slow, and I'm telling you this isn't necessary."

I press the gas pedal a little harder to pick up speed. I only wanted to make sure I didn't jostle her too much in case her ankle is in fact broken. "Whether or not you think that isn't my problem." Crap that came out harsher than I intended. "What I mean to say is Angie asked me to take you so I am. But I don't think it's just because you may have broken your ankle, it's also an insurance thing. You got hurt while on the job and she wants to make sure you're okay."

"I guess she has a point. She did end up going to this place whenever she got knocked to the ground earlier this year."

"Wait, what?" How does that even happen? Angie is kind, but she is also mighty and isn't easily pushed around.

"A couple of guys were acting like idiots and she stepped between them and got knocked out."

I think back to last night and the jerks who were giving Delilah a hard time. "Is that something you will deal with a lot?"

"No," she sighs, "well maybe. I'm still pretty new, so I didn't actually see the thing with Angie. But my friend Lisa told me all about it. It seems like when the renovation started happening, all the jerks in our county came out to play."

Speaking of...right now would be a good time to broach the subject plaguing my mind since I was here earlier today. "Is there going to be a problem with me working with you?"

"W—why do you say that?"

"Just the look you made when Eric mentioned it."

"It won't be a problem." I watch her reflection in the rearview mirror. Her face says otherwise. "Oh, look," She points out the window as I'm slowing down, "we're here."

I park as close as possible to the front door, and get out. Pulling open the back door. I grab her hand to help her scoot backward out of the car. With a bit of maneuvering, she's standing by my side.

"Do you need help getting inside?"

She shivers when a gust of wind whips around the corner. "I think I got it."

I lean in and grab one of my hoodies, sniffing it before I hand it to her. "Here. And it's no problem. I won't stay in there with you if you don't want me to, but at least let me help get you to the nurse's station."

"Fine." She huffs as she puts my hoodie over her head, "let me see your phone."

"Why?"

She holds her hand out without another word mentioned. I pull my phone out of my pocket and unlock it before handing it over. She punches in a number and hits call. Her phone lights up less than a second later.

"Now I have your number for when I get out." She gives me back my phone and hobbles toward the door without waiting for my assistance. Angie was right. She does not like asking for help.

8

delilah

I MAKE it inside the care center before he can help. In hindsight, I probably should have accepted his help. My ankle is throbbing from the weight I put on it. I didn't think it would be that bad since it's a short distance. I was wrong.

"Hi, how can we help you?" the woman at the desk asks.

"I need to get my ankle checked out," I look down at my shoeless foot, "it's either badly sprained or broken."

"Oh, yes," she looks down at her desk, "I have a message from your boss, Angie, right here." Grabbing a few forms and attaching them to a clipboard, she hands them to me through the window. "Just have a seat, fill these out, and we'll have you in a room shortly."

"Thanks." I lift a pen out of a coffee cup, and take the clipboard to a seat in front of the windows. A part of me wants to be able to see outside. See what Bryce is doing to kill time while waiting for me. The other part doesn't want to look at him because it will bring up past feelings. And I can't have that. Not if I'm going to guard my heart against him.

I've barely filled out half the forms when they call my name. Placing the clipboard in the seat next to me, I stand, doing my best not to put all my weight on my injured foot. Wincing, I bend over and grab the clipboard.

The nurse approaches me. "I can bring a wheelchair if it'll make things easier."

My ankle screams in pain as I turn and face her. "That's not necessary."

She must see the abject horror on my face because she doesn't push the subject. However, she walks close to me as we make our way to the patient rooms. "It's the first door to the right."

It takes forty-five minutes for them to x-ray my foot and poke around, causing it to hurt so much more than it did before, until they have an answer for me.

"Well Delilah," the doctor makes a few notes in his notepad, "the good news is it's not broken."

I'm terrified to ask, but here goes. "And what's the bad news?"

"The bad news is you need to wear a boot for at least four weeks, then re-evaluate."

No, no. This can't be happening. "I can't be in a boot for almost a month. I have a job where I stand ninety percent of the time."

"Well, you can either take off work for that amount of time. Or you can find a way to do your job without standing as much."

"And what about driving?"

I feel like the four tiny sterile walls in this room are caving in on me. Please don't let him have more bad news. "For the first week or two, I would suggest having someone drive for you." He can tell I'm about to argue, and he would be right. "But you don't have to do it forever. Only until you get used to wearing the boot."

Dammit. I'm almost certain my brother wouldn't have a problem with taking me back and forth to work. Unless, of course, he has band rehearsals, or he's in his room with his writing muse. That could be a problem.

"Okay," I breathed out, "I guess fix me up with the boot and I'll be on my way."

"And crutches."

"And crutches," I mutter under my breath. Because why wouldn't I need something to help me get around?

"Give me a few minutes and I'll be back with both things. Then you can head home."

He walks out of the room and the only thing filling the silence is the hum of the air conditioner going full blast. Although, I don't know why they don't have the heater on because it's cold outside the last time I checked. So much for hoping this was a small sprain that could be fixed up with bandages and ice. This is one of the busiest times of the year, and we're opening up the stage area, and I won't be able to walk.

There's a soft knock on the door before the doctor comes in and sets the crutches on the bed beside me. "Let me get this boot on your foot, and you can be on your merry way."

"Don't I have to pay?" Not that I can afford it, but it's a necessity at this point.

"Nope, the girls up front said it's already taken care of."

"Oh, thanks?" There's only one person who could've taken care of the bill and that's Angie. When I get to work, we're going to have words.

The doctor leaves the room and I stand, and unevenly thanks to my boot, and grab the crutches. Setting each one under my arms, I hobble out of the room, down the hall, toward the front door. Bryce is already there, waiting for me.

"How did you know I was done?"

"I didn't," he holds the door open for me. "I was standing

outside because I told you I wouldn't hover, and the nurse behind the desk told me I needed to get inside because it was too cold and I was going to get sick."

"Well, she's not entirely wrong about that." He's wearing a jacket on top of the hoodie he was wearing when he brought me here. He must've been standing outside for quite a while before the nurses told him to come inside. I can still feel the coolness on the fabric of his jacket as I brush past him.

The wind has picked up and I'm not prepared for it to sting my face, even though the patient room wasn't exactly warm.

"Any chance you can take me back to the bar?" It's not like he can tell me no. He's not my boss, and I need to get to my car. Surely it won't be that hard to maneuver a gas pedal with a boot.

"No can do. I'm under strict orders to take you home." He hurries in front of me to open the car door.

"Excuse me, what?" I try my hardest not to cuss, but the urge to do is almost overwhelming. "Who told you to take me home?"

He waits until I'm in the car before going around and getting in on the driver's side. "Angie," he starts the car and looks over at me, "before you get mad, your car is fine. She called your brother and he's going to pick it up and bring it to you."

"And what about my things?"

"We're going to stop by and Angie will bring it out. She doesn't want you trying to work when you've just gotten out."

"And you're the person she appointed to cart me around?"

"To be fair, I offered. And I'll help you however I can." When I don't say anything, he looks over at me before pulling onto the street. "Seriously, Delilah, if you need anything you only need to call."

"Why?" It's something I need an answer to. "You went

from not even knowing who I am, even though you were close to my brother, to working at the same place I am, to helping me with this injury. I'd like to think it's out of the goodness of your heart, but it's hard to believe in coincidences."

He doesn't say anything, and I know it's because he won't give me an honest answer. But he turns into the first lot we come across and puts the car in park before facing me.

9

bryce

I DON'T KNOW why I'm wasting my time trying to explain myself. She's right. Until last night, I didn't know she existed. But that's on me.

Her eyes are wide with my attention focused on her. "You can think what you want. I was already talking to my sister about applying here before I even went to the bar for our drinks. Secondly, I do remember you, vaguely. Devin would talk about you, but since you didn't hang out in the circles I did, I didn't think anything of it." I take a breath because she's making me face my past ego. "Lastly, I'm helping you because it's the decent thing to do. I can't help if you fell off the ladder when I showed up. But I have experience with injuries, and it's always better to be safe than sorry."

Delilah relaxes, but only a tiny bit. "How do you know about injuries?"

"Seriously? I played football all throughout school. I've gotten injured quite a few times." I shake my head, remembering the days I thought I was invincible and everyone worshipped the ground I walked on. I'm hoping my nephew doesn't turn out that way. "I also went to school for anything I could do with sports tied in."

"Oh." Now that she looks more at ease and less likely to rip my head off, I put the car in drive and head toward the bar. I already told Angie we were on our way, but didn't anticipate this small detour. "Wait. So, why are you wanting a job at Out of the Ashes if you have a degree in something you enjoy?"

This feels a little personal considering the way she's treated me every time I've seen her today. And it's not something I'm ready to talk about because I don't know what the hell I'm going to do. "You might want to let Angie know we're about to pull up."

It's not a graceful subject change, but it'll do...for now. I have a feeling this isn't something she's going to let go. Especially now that I've become intriguing to her. That's one thing I remember Devin saying about his sister. She was curious, and needed to know all the answers.

She seems to take the hint, and pulls her phone out of her pocket. "Thank you for the hoodie by the way." The comment is soft and I barely hear it.

"You're welcome."

The ride is silent other than the holiday music playing softly through the speakers, giving me time to think. If we're being honest, I don't know why I'm trying to get to know her. I don't know what I want to do with my life, and I'm not really in a place to be making decisions with a love life. Besides, she runs hot and cold. And that's just in the twenty-four hours I've known who she is. Hell, I don't know why I'm even infatuated with her. Maybe it's the mystery of this person I could've known this entire time? Either way, I want to know more about her...even if she has a reason to hate me.

I pull into the parking lot of the bar and don't bother trying to find a space. Circling around, I pull up to the curb.

People are giving me dirty looks, but I don't care. It's not like we'll be here for long, or going in for that matter. It's a couple of minutes before Eric comes outside with Delilah's bag.

I push the button to roll down the passenger side window, and Delilah reaches her hand out. "Thanks. It looks packed in there."

"Don't worry about that," he waves the comment away, "get some rest, and I'll see both of you tomorrow." He turns back toward the building, and starts walking, but not before I hear him call back, "Don't do anything I wouldn't do."

"I swear that man is a menace," Delilah sighs and opens her bag, as I inch forward and make my way out of the lot. "One of these days he's going to mind his own business."

"Didn't he play a part in my sister and Carlos getting together?"

"Yeah, even though I told him to leave it alone. He doesn't listen."

That's good information to know. And if she decides I'm more than a nuisance, I might have to enlist his help. "Which way do I go?" I know when we were in school, they lived on the opposite side of town from us. My mom would pick Devin up for early morning practices, and I hated how early I'd have to wake up.

"Left." She points in the same direction. As if I don't understand the word she just said. "It's not far from here. Maybe ten minutes."

I do as instructed and turn left. Shockingly enough, this is the same direction I live. We're getting closer to my house and I'm worried she's forgotten to tell me where to turn, but two streets before mine, she says to take a right.

"You know, I actually live a couple of streets over."

"Oh, I figured you'd be in your own place." So, she knows where I live. Or, where my mom lives since, they seem to have a close relationship I didn't know about.

"Kind of hard to do that without a job," I laugh. Acting as if the comment doesn't sting. It seems like a shortcoming, and I hate doing anything less than the best when it comes to my life. It's the reasons giving up football in college to be able to help my mom and sister was so hard.

"You'll be on your feet in no time," she says it so matter of factly. "My house is coming up."

She points to the left and I start slowing down. "This one?"

"Yep." Shoving her phone in her bag, she starts zipping things up. It's small. Maybe two bedrooms at most. I'm surprised she lives in a house and not an apartment. At least she has her own place.

I park in the driveway and turn off the car. She has her bag and crutches to get out, and I can't let her do that on her own. She opens her door, grabs the crutches and sets them outside the car. Damn, she's quick.

Getting out the car, I rush to her side. "Let me hold your bag."

"You don't have to do that."

"Humor me." Reluctantly, she hands me the bag. I pull the crutches from where she set them, and hold them out in front of her. "I'll let go when you're steady."

She moves until both of her feet are hanging out of the car, and pulls her hands further into the sleeves of the hoodie until they are covered. Scooting forward, she places the uninjured foot on the ground and stands. Her booted foot lifted in the air until she gets the crutches in a comfortable spot. "Okay, I'm ready."

Letting go of the crutches, I take a step to the side, giving her space to maneuver. She slowly moves away from the car, and I close the car door from behind her. I do my best to block the wind as I walk. "Do you have your house key? I can unlock it for you."

"They are in the front pocket of my bag."

I reach in until my fingers grasp around the warm metal. Once we get to the door, I unlock it and move to the side so she can go inside. It's gotten colder since we left the urgent care facility and lingering on the porch makes me feel like a creeper, but she didn't invite me in. I'm not going to assume I should follow her.

Instead, I set the bag inside her door, and wait for her to remember I'm here. "I guess I'll see you later." I wave awkwardly and take a step back.

"Do you want to come inside?" That is the absolute last question I thought she'd ask.

10

delilah

I DON'T KNOW why I just asked him to come in. It's like something came over me and threw the words out of my mouth. Now that they are out there, I can't take them back. Can't rescind the invite because that would be rude, and if my mom knew I did that, she'd be all over my butt.

"Are you sure?" he asks and shoves his hands into the front pocket on his hoodie.

He's giving me a way out without being rude, but he has gone above and beyond to help me tonight when nobody asked. The least I can do is offer to feed him, or give him a bottle of water. Not like I have much food, but frozen pizzas can be cooked pretty quickly.

"Yeah, I'm sure."

He takes a slow step inside and closes the door behind him. I try to take a step backward, forgetting I have crutches holding me up, and almost fall. Just like earlier, Bryce is there to catch me. It makes it very difficult to keep my distance, and my heart safe, when he keeps doing these things. Maybe he isn't as self-centered as I thought he was. Or, maybe he grew up. I don't know, but I'm starting to feel like I want to find out.

"Woah." His arms are around my waist, and he's hold me up. My crutches now on the floor below me. "I have a feeling; crutches are going to be fun for you. Do I need to stick around all the time to make sure you don't bust up your other ankle?"

I laugh and grab onto his shoulders to help him keep me stable. "I'm beginning to wonder if you aren't the universal cause of my sudden clumsiness."

Bryce adjusts one of his arms, moving it to my upper back. He bends down and the other arm falls to the back of my knees. Before I know what's happening, he's lifting me up, cradling me, as he carries me to the small sofa against the wall. He sets me down and backs away. "You should be pretty safe right here."

"Thanks. Obviously, I'm a safety hazard to myself and everyone else."

"No, you aren't." He walks toward the entry way and grabs the crutches off the floor. "Where do you want me to put these?"

"I guess over here by me. Not that they will do me much good. I can't seem to walk on them."

He brings them to the side of the sofa I'm sitting on. "It's not too hard once you get the hang of it. I've had to use them more times than I'd like. How long do you have to use them?"

I think back to my conversation with the doctor. "Actually, I'm not sure. I forgot to ask the doc. Hopefully it's not too long because I'll be the cause of injuries to all of you."

"Naw," he grins, "may I?" As soon as I nod, he takes a seat next to me. "You'll get it, and it'll feel weird when you no longer have to use them. You need them for the first few days, maybe a week at most, until the swelling goes down. Then you can walk around with only the boot."

"How do you know all this?"

"School." He pauses for a second, debating what he wants to say. Maybe he'll talk about why he's working at the bar. "Well, school and life experience. But I learned how to deal with injuries related to sports while at school. I'd like to coach at the high school, but apparently you have to have a teaching certificate for that to happen."

"You didn't know that when you chose your major?" It's odd that he wouldn't, but I decided not to go the college route. It didn't appeal to me.

"No, Coach told me at my nephew's last game of the season." He leans his head on the back of the sofa. "There are multiple jobs I could do instead, but this is what I really want to do."

"You know there are other ways to coach kids, right?"

"What do you mean?"

Has he really not thought of this before? "You can coach at one of the organizations for kids, or even do private coaching. I'm sure there are a lot of parents who would like a state champion quarterback to teach their children how to play."

"Hmm, I never thought of that," he turns to face me, "how do you know we won state?"

"My brother, remember?"

"Oh, yeah," he rolls his eyes, "did you ever come to the games?"

Shaking my head, I lift my foot onto the table in front of me. "They weren't really my thing."

The room is silent and it's an odd feeling. Usually, I have the TV on, or music streaming, to keep from feeling so alone after Lisa moved out. Well, some of her stuff is still here, but I refuse to put it in storage for her because I know she'll be back. Even if she doesn't call as much as she used to.

I glance at my phone and realize it's almost midnight. "Do you want some—" The words die on my lips because when I look over at Bryce, his eyes are closed and his mouth is hanging open. How in the hell do guys fall asleep so quickly? Do they not have a million things running through their mind when they close their eyes? It's a secret I don't think I'll ever have the answer to.

Pulling the blanket from behind me, I do my best to lay it across him without waking him up. As much as he's waiting on me today, the least I can do is let him get some sleep. If he works the night shifts at the bar this is something he won't be able to do as much.

I move toward the edge of the sofa and push myself onto my feet. Even through the padding of the wrap and boot, I wince putting weight on my foot. Not wanting to wake Bryce, I forego the crutches. This may be painful for now, but I just want to fall into my bed. It's been a long, and weird day.

Doing my best not to stomp, I shuffle to my room. The thought of taking off the boot and unraveling the wrap is too much for my level of exhaustion, and I fall onto the bed still in my clothes. My eyes close instantly.

My phone dinging wakes me up, and I glance at my phone. What? How is it already morning? It feels like I just closed my eyes. Apparently hurting myself requires a lot of sleep. Wiping my eyes, I swipe it open to see who it is.

DEVIN

Who just left your house?

11

bryce

SHIT. This is most definitely not my bed. I glance around Delilah's living room. I can't believe I fell asleep on her couch. In the middle of a conversation no less. Who even does that?

She's nowhere to be seen, but her crutches are sitting exactly where I left them. Did she go to bed without them? If so, she has to be in pain. There's a possibility she also fell asleep on the couch, and is moving around. I listen for a few minutes. There's no sound coming from anywhere in the house.

My phone is in my pocket, and I pull it out to check the time. The screen is full of notifications from my mom, Angie, and my siblings. Mom must be worried sick, and I get off the couch as quickly, and quietly, as possible. My steps are light as I head toward the door. After opening it, I lock the door from the inside and then close it behind me.

The only thing working for me right now is the fact I live a couple of streets over. There's no point calling my mom when I can see her in two minutes. I click the unlock button on the key fob and rush to my car. She probably thinks the worst since she knew I was heading to the bar and then didn't come home. Getting in the car, I start the engine and don't bother waiting for it to warm up before pulling out of Delilah's driveway.

I pass one car as I make my way down the street before turning on the main intersection. Most people are already at work, or they don't go in until later. I'm pretty sure Mom has today off. Even if she didn't, I doubt she'd go in until she heard from me. She's overprotective like that. She still calls Caroline and Reaf when she knows they are going out. As annoying as it can be, I'm glad she cares.

Her car is still in the driveway when I pull up beside it. I turn the car off, duck inside my hoodie and rush up the porch steps. The door's locked which means Mom did go to bed at some point last night.

When I walk through the door, she jolts up from the chair. Her hair going in a million different directions. "Where the hell have you been?"

"I'm so sorry, Mom."

"Seriously, I've held my phone in my hand all night expecting the worst news to come through the other end."

Wow. I didn't realize my being gone freaked her out that much. What did she do the entire time I was away at college? I mean, I was home a lot on the weekends, but I was gone a majority of the time.

"I really am sorry. I forgot to let you know what was going on. Delilah hurt herself at work while I was turning in my application and I volunteered to take her to the doctor to get checked out."

"Oh no," Mom gasps. "Is she okay?"

Nodding, I sit on the couch opposite from her. "Yeah, she's in a boot for a few weeks minimum, but overall, she's fine." I probably shouldn't ask this, but I think my mom has a decent relationship with her, and I want to know. "Why doesn't Delilah like me very much?"

She looks everywhere but at me. "Why would you ask that?"

"Because she runs hot and cold with me. Mostly cold, though. Did I unintentionally do something to her?" It's been bugging me since her reaction the other night, and I need to know. Last night seemed like we were making progress. At least, enough for her to talk to me without a scowl on her face.

"It's not really my place to tell."

"Please, Mom. I need to know what I can do to make it right. We'll be working together and it'll make things so much easier...for both of us."

She places her hands in her lap. Fingers tapping while she decides what she will, and won't, say. "Fine. But only because I want the two of you to get along." She takes a deep breath, "she had a crush on you in high school. She'll probably never admit it, but I could tell. It's a mother's instinct to know when someone likes her child. The reason she doesn't seem like your biggest fan is because as you proved the other night, you didn't know who she was. You were at her house when you hung out with Devin, and she was invisible to you."

It's not like I went over there that often. He mostly came here, alone. And when I was at their house, we were either in his room or outside throwing the football. "I've already apologized for that."

"Actions speak louder, Bryce. But I think helping her out yesterday is a step in the right direction. She is probably keeping her guard up to make sure you aren't going to unintentionally hurt her again." She stands and groans, "I cannot sleep in this chair again. My body is way too old for it."

That's something I definitely need to remember. Not the chair part, but the actions. And the fact I hurt her without even knowing it. Maybe she was lying when she said she didn't come to the games. I do remember that being the last thing we talked about before I passed out. "I'll get some coffee going for you. I'm sure Angie will be waiting for me to check in with her, and I need to see what my schedule is."

She nods and heads toward her room. I feel bad for making her worry, but I'm glad she's the understanding type.

Next step, making Delilah realize she doesn't hate me, and could possibly go out on a date with me. Back then I was stupid. I'd like to think I've grown up since, but she needs to see that. My new goal is proving that to her, no matter what it takes.

After that, I'll figure out what I'm doing with my life. Delilah had some good suggestions, but I don't know if my heart would be in those as much as it would be to coach older kids. To help them reach their dreams to play in college, and beyond.

For now, I'll make my mom's coffee. The pods are almost gone and I'll need to go to the store and get more. It's the least I can do after the stress I put her through last night.

My phone vibrates in my pocket, and I pull it out to check it.

DELILAH

Can I ask you for a favor?

Instead of typing out a response, I press her name and call her.

12

delilah

MY PHONE RINGS seconds after sending the text. What the crap? He was supposed to text back, not call me. If I don't answer it soon, it's going to roll over to voicemail. He's throwing off my entire energy. Screw it. I tap answer, "hello?"

"Hey." He's smiling, I can tell by the way his voice sounds. It's how it always sounded when he was happy in high school. You'd think I'd forget that after four years, but no. "What kind of favor do you need?"

A part of me doesn't want to ask him, but he's my only option since my brother is being a jerk. To say he was shocked to learn it was Bryce who was leaving my house this morning is an understatement. He also decided that since we work together and Bryce lives just around the corner, I could ask him.

"Is there anyway you can give me a ride to and from work until I can drive?" It's not an ideal situation, but it's the best I can come up with. So much for keeping my walls up. He's already begun pulling them down, but spending more time with him is no doubt going to make them crash to the floor. I know he's planning on sticking around the area, but what if he changes his mind. Worse...what if I'm a conquest to fulfill a curiosity.

"Sure. I was about to call Angie and see what my schedule is."

"Don't."

"Why?"

"There's a good chance she isn't even awake yet. She's not exactly an early riser." That's an understatement. It's why she doesn't require us to be in until ten thirty at the earliest. We open right around lunch time, and it's all because she doesn't want to get up after a long night working the bar.

"Good to know." He pauses for a second and I hear movement in the background. "You may have just saved my job."

"What are you doing?" There's hissing sounds now.

"Sorry." Something thuds. He's definitely a noisy phone talker. "I'm making coffee for my mom. Apparently not checking in last night caused her to freak out the entire time."

"Are you serious?"

"Yeah. I didn't realize I needed to do that."

He does not think things through. "It's a courtesy thing, especially since you're living there again." I still let my parents know when I'll be out later than expected. But maybe that's something girls do and guys don't. It's a safety precaution for me, and makes me feel better when they know what's going on. Sometimes I even let my brother know. With some of the people that come into the bar, it's never a bad idea to be cautious.

"That makes sense. It's hard getting into new habits after I've been on my own for so long."

"Understandable." The line is silent, and I don't know what to say to fill the void. I barely know him, even though I lusted after him most of the time we were in school. This is getting weird.

I'm about to let him go when he asks, "Are you hungry?"

That's a good question. I didn't eat anything after falling off the ladder. Looking back, it's such a cringe-worthy moment. Like all those feel-good movies they show during the holidays. It's the perfect meet cute, but I already know Bryce...sort of. Now, I want to get to know him better, and not the cocky jerk he was in school. "Yeah, I could definitely eat."

"How long will it take you to get ready?"

"Not long."

"Awesome. I'll be there in twenty."

"Okay." I look down at yesterday's clothes I'm still wearing. "I'll be ready."

It's a good thing I took a shower yesterday before work because I don't know if I can figure out the shower with a hurt foot in less than twenty minutes. It might take me that long to get the wrapping on it done. Or maybe I can wait until Bryce gets here, and he can show me how to do it.

* * *

There's a knock at the door, and I do my best to adjust the crutches and make it there in a decent amount of time. I'd like to say I'm getting the hang of it, but they keep throwing off my balance. Taking my time, so I don't fall on my butt again, I make it to the door and open it. "Hey."

"Where's your boot?" Of course, that's the first thing he notices. I'm not sure if it's a dig or if he's actually concerned.

"I was in too much shock over having to wear it that I wasn't paying attention with how he wrapped it. Any chance you can show me?"

"Sure thing." He waits for me to turn around and move

from in front of the door before he comes inside, giving me space to. "Do you have the wrap in here?"

"Crap," I slap my hand on my forehead, "it's in my room. Give me a few minutes to grab it."

"You sit," he commands, "point in the right direction and I'll get it."

I do as he says, and lower myself on the sofa before setting my crutches to the side. I've at least got that part figured out. "It's straight down the hall at the end. All of it should be on the bed."

"Be right back." He hurries down the hall and back before I know it. Huh, he didn't take the opportunity to linger, or check out my room. He's either respecting my privacy, or he's really hungry. If I had to guess, it's the latter.

He sits on the floor in front of me, and rubs his hands together. "Let me see your foot." Moving my right foot toward him, he pushes the table to give him some room. He gently touches my foot and asks, "Are my hands too cold?"

"N-no, they're fine." A single touch from him should not spur this sort of reaction. It shouldn't make me want him to move his hand higher, and yet it does. Getting to know him, and getting to know him are two separate things, and my heart isn't ready for the second no matter how much my body disagrees.

"Okay, I'm going to lift the edge of your leggings a bit for better access." One hand cradles my foot, and the other slowly pushes the bottom of my leggings up. I should have taken a shower this morning. I can't even remember the last time I shaved, and he has to be feeling the prickles of the new grown hair. As if falling from a ladder, and tripping over my own crutches, wasn't embarrassing enough. Let's add this to the mix.

He grabs the jumbled mess of wrapping and does his best to straighten it out before placing it on the side of my foot.

His touch is gentle as he places it around my ankle, under my foot, and back around. The pattern methodical as if he's done it a thousand times, which he probably has. I'm doing my best to keep my breathing under control. I know this is for medical reasons, but I don't think anyone has taken that much care in how they touch me. Except him.

Within a few minutes he has my ankle wrapped and is slipping the boot onto my foot. I wiggle it around to make sure it's not uncomfortable. It's not too tight or loose. Perfect. "Thank you."

"No problem." He stands and grabs my crutches. "Are you ready to go?"

"Absolutely." I push my pants leg down and stand. He hands me the crutches before grabbing the jacket he sees on the hook by the door. He waits until I'm steady on my feet and slides the jacket on my arms. "Thanks."

Who knew this side of him existed? I definitely didn't, but I can't wait to find out more.

13

bryce

I HAVE to say this new routine isn't bad at all. Not only do I get to spend more time getting to know Delilah, but I also have a job that I like. For now, at least. I still want to coach, but this is a nice little break after all the time I've spent in school. It's also keeping me occupied instead of sitting at home trying to figure out what my next move will be.

Angie decided to put me and Delilah on the same shift since I'm her ride to work and home. That could change once Delilah is able to drive. Right now, I'll relish in the time I get to spend with her.

Today, we're on the day shift. Delilah is sitting on a stool Angie brought from her house so Delilah isn't on her feet as much. She's already starting to improve. I've noticed the swelling has gone down each time I've wrapped it. "Eric," she yells across the bar, "I need you to make sure the tables are spread out far enough outside the dance floor."

"You've gotten bossy since your injury," he fires back.

"I was like this before you just don't listen." She grins at me. "Can you make sure he does it right? If it looks too crowded take some out. The whole point of the stage is to give people a concert feel while in a smaller establishment."

"You got it." I take my time walking into the newer area of the bar to keep Eric from thinking I'm there to babysit him. Even though, that's kind of what she told me to do since nobody is here for the lunch rush, yet. "Need some help?"

"I don't need you to watch over me. Despite what she thinks, I'm capable of carrying out a small task."

"I have no doubt, but have you tried telling her no?" It's not even so much that she gives out orders. It's the sweet, wide-eyed expression she gives when asking, or telling, you to do something. It'd be like telling a kid no when they ask for their favorite snack.

"You have a point," he points toward the other side of the room, "you start over there. Most of them are okay, but a few need to be moved out further."

"On it." The decorations in here match what is in the front half of the space, and I move around them to get to the tables. I'm not sure this was the smartest idea. From what everyone says Stella knows what she's doing, but this seems like asking for trouble when a bunch of drunk people are in the throes of musical bliss.

I lift the table at the end of the row and move it down, spreading my arms out to make sure there's space for people to move around. I'm caught off guard when Eric pops up behind me. "So, what are your intentions with Delilah? Do you actually like her, or are you going to play her?"

"What do you mean?" This is coming out of left field for me.

"I see the way you look at each other. She also filled me in on some things from high school," he looks behind him to make sure nobody can overhear us. "She's like a sister to me since I've started working here, and I'll do whatever I need to in order to protect her heart. Or, help her see what's right in front of her." He points his finger at my chest, "you are the deciding factor on which way that support goes."

This could work. It's also good to know he's got her back no matter which way this conversation goes. I wish my sister had someone besides her family in her corner when it came to her ex-husband. It really makes all the difference.

"Would you judge who you are now based on your past?"

He laughs, "Hell no. I was an asshole when I was a teen. I can be now, but that's beside the point."

"Okay then," I grin, "I'm also capable of change. The way she stepped in to help me that night when I would have made an ass of myself was refreshing. I didn't know we went to school together." It also proved how much of an egotistical asshole I was in school. I was in my own little world with football and didn't care about anything else. "I want to rectify any pain I caused in the past. She seems to be warming up to me."

"That's all I needed to hear." He slaps me on the back, "now get those chairs moved over and see what else we need to do to get ready for the grand opening of the stage this weekend."

"Will do." I get the chairs pushed into the table I moved moments ago. This place is going to be better than ever once that opens up. People won't have to go to the closest city for live music anymore.

Delilah is standing at the podium when I make my way to the main bar area. "Bryce, can you show them to a table?" She motions toward the couple in front of her. It's Mr. Jones and his wife. It's amazing to see the two of them still go on dates after all these years. He's well past retirement age and still works because he refuses to let go of his rental company.

"Absolutely." I nod my head for them to follow me. I can feel Delilah's eyes on me, and it's good to know that she seems to be interested. "Is this booth okay?" He nods his affirmation and they both sit on the same side. "Here's the menu, and I'll be back to take your order."

"No need for that. We know what we want." He waves my comment away. He gives me his order and as soon as I'm done writing it down, he taps the menu on the table. "Be sure to keep her around. She's a good one."

"What do you mean?"

"Delilah. She's had her eye on you since we came through the door."

"I'll keep that in mind." I pull the paper off the notepad. "I'll be back with your drinks."

Before I even make it to the bar to request the drinks, Delilah is walking toward me as fast as she can. "Why do they keep looking at me?"

Shrugging, I grin. "I have no idea." It's a lie, and she knows it. She isn't pushing, though. "Do you know what else we need to do for the grand opening?"

"No, but Angie has the list in her office." She shakes her head at my subject change. "I'll just be over there making sure we have everything we need for our Christmas party."

"You do that." I take a step back and pause. This is my chance. "Are you bringing a plus one?"

"No. I was thinking about asking Devin, but I think he's getting everything ready to perform for the opening. Why?"

Huh, so he really decided to go down the musician path. I could never do it, but good for him. "Well, I'm not bringing anyone, and if you're not bringing anyone, maybe we could go together?"

"We're already driving together." She rolls her eyes.

"I mean like a date."

This time she laughs and slaps her leg before wincing. I guess someone forgot not to step on her bad ankle. "I'm not opposed to a date with you, but our work party is not going to be the first one."

"Fair enough," I put my hands up in surrender. "Hope you don't have any plans after work because I'm taking you out."

14

delilah

HE WALKS AWAY to put the food order in before I have a chance to say anything. Did he really just say all of that loud enough for everyone to hear? He's smooth. And I did kind of agree to a date. It could be a huge mistake, but he doesn't seem like the self-centered jerk he was back then. People change, and I'm open to giving them a second chance. Lord knows I've done it enough with friendships. Even if I ended up getting burned in those. Everything will work out. It has to.

My boot makes a loud thud with every step I take toward the podium. I don't have time to worry about that. I need to check on the catering for our party and panic about the date it appears I'm having tonight. I wonder if there's a way to wiggle out of it.

"So, you're going on a date tonight?" Eric leans on the podium.

"Shouldn't you be doing something, like making drinks?" He always has to insert himself. He's not cupid. Though he seems to think he is. Maybe he was in a past life, and he goes hard for relationships he can push together.

"I've already done that. It's not like there's a ton of people here." He glances over at Mr. Jones and looks back at me. "In fact, I only count two."

"Obviously." I expect him to go back to the bar and make himself busy, but he doesn't. He's waiting for an answer, and I don't know if I want to give him that ammo. "Is there anything else?"

"I just need to know if you're going to change before you go out. I mean, you look cute and all," he waves his arm up and down over what I'm wearing, "but nothing about that says date."

"This," I lift up my booted foot, "makes it difficult to dress cute. It doesn't exactly scream hot date."

"At least go with something that doesn't look like a work uniform."

Rolling my eyes, I shoo him away. "Spend less time worrying about my love life, and more time working. I have things I need to do."

"Fine," he backs away, "but give the guy an honest chance. He's not so bad."

"Go away." Him and Bryce must have talked, but he has nothing to worry about, I fully intend on giving him a shot.

* * *

"Is there anywhere in particular you'd like to go?" Bryce asks as he helps me into the car. He dropped me off after work so we could both get ready. According to him, he smelled like food and spilled booze. He wasn't entirely wrong.

He opens the back door and slides my crutches onto the backseat. I don't answer until he's back in the driver seat.

"Aren't you supposed to have this figured out? You're the one who asked me on a date."

"Well, yeah, but that was before you agreed." He puts the car in reverse and backs out of my driveway. "Is there any sort of foods you don't like?"

I feel like I should be offended that he thought I might say no, but I don't blame him. Our first few interactions weren't exactly great, and I was still holding him at arm's length. I can understand his apprehension. "Fish. That's it. I like seafood as long as it isn't fish."

"You realize that makes zero sense, right?" He laughs. It's deep and carefree. Even though I know he's battling with what he wants to do with his life, he still enjoys every moment he can. I wasn't expecting that. My brother is carefree, but he's also very serious when it comes to his music. It's amazing how the two of them used to be friends, but they've both turned into different people.

"It makes perfect sense." I turn toward him, "it's all about the texture. Shrimp and foods like that have a meatier feel. Fish, just falls apart as soon as you bite it and it weirds me out."

"I'll give you that." He turns the music up loud enough to be heard, but not so loud it drowns out our conversation. "So, I'd be safe taking you to a steakhouse?"

"Yes. That's always a safe bet."

"If all goes well, we can always hang out at my house afterward. Watch a movie or something?"

He's already planning for after the date. How does he know he'll want anything to do with me outside of friendship? I'll roll with it, though. It's something Lisa told me before she left. Take opportunities, even if they scare you. "Or, we could watch movies at my place. It makes more sense, and you won't have to go back and forth."

Besides, I know his mom took pity on me at graduation,

and she picked up on my crush. It would feel weird being there with him until I know how this date goes.

"Good idea."

The car is silent aside from the music and heater. He's going toward the new steakhouse downtown and I'm surprised he's taking me someplace so expensive for our first date.

I glance over at him as he's pulling into the parking lot, and he's mouthing words. It takes a few seconds for it to dawn on me, but he's silently singing the words to the song on the radio. "I didn't take you for a Mariah Carey fan."

His mouth snaps shut. "I don't know what you're talking about."

"It's okay. No judgement here. The holiday season is a vibe, and if people want to belt Christmas music, that's fine by me."

He parks the car and turns toward me. "Please don't tell anyone. Do you have any idea how much shit my brother and sister will give me if they find out?"

"Your secret is safe with me." I mime zipping my mouth shut and throwing away the key.

"Thank you," he sighs. You'd think being the baby of the family, he would get away with whatever he wants. But I've met both of his siblings. They are sweet as can be, but love to tease those they love. "Do you want me to get your crutches from the back?"

I glance in the back seat. "No, I think I'll be okay without them." And I will. It's getting easier to move around with only the boot. Plus, I don't want to be the one people are staring at as I walk into the restaurant.

"Okay, but they are here if you need them."

"I know."

He turns off the car, and gets out before coming to my door. He helps me get out of the car, but leaves his arm out once the door is closed. After locking the car, he leans into me. "You can hold onto my arm if you need to."

"Thank you."

He hasn't started walking, and I don't understand why not. "I forgot to say it earlier, but you look beautiful tonight."

I can feel my cheeks redden. "Thank you."

He's pulling out all the stops tonight and I know despite my fears, my heart is all in.

15

bryce

DINNER WAS A SUCCESS. Well, as far as I can tell. She didn't take back her offer inviting me over. I'm calling that a win. And holy crap, I didn't realize how expensive that place was. Carlos mentioned that it was one of his favorites to take my sister to for date night, but I think he forgot I just finished college. I'm not exactly drowning in money. It was worth it though. The food. The company. Everything was perfect.

"What movie do you want to watch?" Delilah pulls me out of my thoughts. "I have most streaming services since my parents still have me on their accounts."

"That depends. Would you make fun of me if I said a cheesy holiday movie?"

She giggles and it might be my new favorite sound. "Not at all. I was secretly hoping you'd say something along those lines. Lisa, my old roommate, used to watch them with me when she was here. It feels weird watching them when I'm alone."

"I guess it's a good thing I'm here." Jesus. Did that just

come out of my mouth? It's like I'm taking the cheesiest thoughts in my mind and saying them instead of something smooth. She is throwing off my usual banter. It's fine, though. She didn't cringe. "I just need to text my mom and let her know I'll be home late."

"Sounds good. I'll get some popcorn. I think I might even have hot chocolate." Okay, so she's into the whole cheese-fest. I can work with that.

"Do you need help?"

"I've got it."

She stands and heads to the kitchen. The crutches are a thing of the past for her. It's not a bad thing, but I'll keep my eye on her just in case. Her mobility with the boot is definitely better than I expected it to be considering it hasn't even been a week.

Pulling my phone out of my pocket, I hit my mom's information to send her a text. I'd call, but that could feel awkward.

BRYCE

Hey mom, just filling you in so you don't spend all night thinking I'm in a ditch. At Delilah's watching movies. I'll be home late.

MOM

Thanks. And if you don't come home, I understand.

BRYCE

Gross

Seriously, I think I just threw up in my mouth a little. I'd expect that from Caroline, but Mom. That may be one of those things where lines should never be crossed. I was happy when she bought me condoms as a teen because I was embarrassed, but to be hinting at my sex life via text...that's just too far.

"Everything okay?" Delilah sets a bowl of popcorn on the table before she returns to the kitchen.

"Uh, yeah. Just my mom being herself." She comes back with a mug in each hand, the liquid close to spilling over. "Here, let me help you with that." I take both mugs from her and set them on either side of the popcorn.

"Anything you'd like to share?"

"Definitely not." The list of holiday movies on the screen is huge. I'm not even sure how far down it goes. "How are we going to pick what movie to watch?"

"We'll leave it to fate."

"What do you mean?"

She picks up the remote and points it toward the TV. "Both of us are going to close our eyes. I'm going to press all the arrows in various order for thirty seconds. Whatever movie the cursor lands on is the one we'll watch."

"What if it sucks?"

"We won't know until we watch it."

I wonder if she makes a lot of decisions like this. If maybe that's how she decided to give me a chance. I'm not knocking it, but if it works...it works. Covering my eyes with my hand, I whisper, "I'm ready."

"Are your eyes closed behind your hand?"

It's a valid question because no they are not closed. But I snap them shut. "They are now."

"All right let's do this." I can hear the remote clicking rapidly, and I'm not sure precisely how much time has passed but this feels like it's taking forever.

"Do we have a winner?" I've never been a huge fan of surprises, but this actually feels nice. I'm excited to see what fate has decided we should watch.

"I think so," she takes a deep breath, "open your eyes on three. One. Two. Three." She squeals before I can open mine. "Yes, I love this movie."

"What is it about?"

"I can't tell you that," she grins. "It'll ruin the movie. Can you grab that blanket?" She points behind me.

"Sure." I lean forward and reach behind me before handing it to her. She lays it across her lap, letting the excess fall between us. "Ready to get this party started?"

She presses play. I grab the bowl of popcorn, setting it between us. "If you like cheesy movies, you'll love this one."

"I guess we'll see." I watch her as she picks up her mug of hot chocolate. She keeps her booted foot on the table and pulls the other leg up until it's tucked underneath. At least that's what I assume happened since her bottom half is covered by a blanket.

She presses play, and I take a sip of my hot chocolate. It even has the little marshmallows in it. Delilah truly is a kid at heart like me. She just doesn't show it. This movie is already starting out weird. Why are there knights? I got lost in watching the girl next to me instead of the TV. It's supposed to be a Christmas movie.

"I think you picked the wrong genre." I whisper to her.

"Just wait."

Okay, I'll wait. Though, right now, I'm not seeing a ton of crossover. After a few more minutes the knight is transported to modern times in the middle of a Christmas festival. Okay, now, it has my attention. Finishing my hot chocolate, I set the mug on the table.

It's getting cooler in here even though I can hear the heater blowing. I wonder if she needs her windows resealed, but I'm not going to ask her that now. Not when she's enraptured with a movie she's already seen. Instead of complaining, I cover my hands with the ends of my sweater and cross my arms. Hopefully it doesn't get much colder than this.

A few moments later she sets her mug on the table, and glances in my direction. "Are you cold?"

"Nah, I'm fine." I uncross my arms and grab a handful of popcorn to prove everything is good.

She lifts the bowl of popcorn, placing it in her lap before lifting the edge of the blanket closest to me. "There's room for you under here. I promise I don't bite."

"I'll be fine, I promise."

She grabs the remote and presses pause. "I'm not turning the movie on until you get under the blanket. I can practically hear your teeth chattering."

"They are not." After a few seconds of thought, I do as she says. Our legs are pressed together once I'm settled beneath the blanket. "Why is it so cold anyway?"

"I try to not to use the heater too much." She looks down as if afraid to admit anything. "It wasn't so bad when I had a roommate, but with her gone, I do everything I can to shave off expenses."

That makes sense. "Tomorrow before we leave for work, I'm going to check your windows to make sure no air is coming through."

"Thank you." I'm glad she isn't fighting me on this. Being next to her is nice. Had I not been a jerk in high school, I could have had this experience years ago.

16

delilah

OH MY GOSH. This is one of the few moments I always imagined when I was a lovestruck teen. And now...now it's happening. I hope I wasn't too forward, but I couldn't think of another reason to get him closer. Honestly, I'm shocked he didn't try to sit right next to me earlier. Maybe the date night hasn't gone the way I imagined, and he's placating me before saying we're better off as friends.

"Are you going to press play?" I can feel his breath against my ear, and it sends a shiver through my body.

"Sorry." I press the button and set the remote on the arm of the sofa. I reach into the bowl of popcorn at the same time as he does and our hands touch. Geez, I feel like a schoolgirl who's never had a boyfriend. But I can't help it. My teenage self would be so happy with this moment.

Don't get ahead of yourself. It's something I keep having to say. Otherwise, I'll get lost in my past infatuation. I'm trying very hard to make sure anything I feel for him is rooted in the present, and not the way I imagined things as a sixteen-year old.

Everything about this moment feels intimate. The same way it does when he wraps my ankle for me. Which is something he does every morning, even though I know how to do it now.

"Are you done with this?" He points toward the popcorn.

"Oh, uh, yeah." It's not a lie. I don't want to have popcorn stuck in my teeth if he tries to kiss me. There's nothing cute about that.

He takes the bowl and sets it on the table. He puts his left arm around my shoulder and his fingers caress my upper arm. There's only one thing I can do...lean into him. It's not easy with the boot on my foot, but I don't want to break the mood trying to take it off.

We both settle into the comfort of each other while watching the movie. This is the closest, both emotionally and physically, I've allowed myself to be with someone in a very long time. It feels right despite this being our first date. Maybe it's the days leading up to tonight that helped, but I feel like I know him.

"What? No!" I jump at the sound of his outburst.

"What's wrong?" I've pretty much zoned out from watching the movie, which is fine since I've already seen it.

"He's going back." He looks down at me, "why is he going back? She's his destiny."

It's cute that he's so worked up over this movie. Who would have thought he'd be into these kinds of movies? Definitely not me. Especially not to the extent he's showing now. "Just keep watching. You know dang well they'll end up together. It wouldn't be a holiday romance without that aspect."

"I know, but does he have to be so dumb with his decision," he shakes his head. "She's right there. They kissed. He felt the same way as her."

My hand closest to him is pinned between us. Meer inches from his, and I debate taking hold. Instead, I lift my other hand and search for his mouth to cover it. "Just. Watch. The. Movie."

He stops his mini rant, and closes his mouth. I remove my hand and set it in my lap. The knight realizes what he's done and makes his way back to his one true love. Bryce moves his hand and moments later interlocks his fingers with mine just as the girl realizes her knight is back. That he chose her. Is this his way of saying he's choosing me? I hope so.

As much as it excites me, it worries me. What happens if he decides the only way to fulfill his passion is to get his teaching certificate? He'll probably leave for school again, and while I'd like to say I'm okay with a long-distance relationship, I know deep down I wouldn't be.

The end credits roll, and I sit up to grab the remote. Bryce lifts my hand in his. "I hope this is okay."

"It is."

"Good. I've wanted to do that since we sat down."

My cheeks warm, and I toss the remote in his lap. "Want to stay a little longer and watch another one?"

"Sure." He grabs the remote and exits to the screen I was searching on. "Do I have to do it the way you do?"

"Not at all." I pull my hand out of his and lean forward. "I'm going to take this off while you decide. Wait," I pause, "is it okay for me to take it off even though I'm still awake?"

"Yep. As long as it's elevated, which it is, you're fine."

He navigates the screen and decides on a movie just as I'm finished pulling off the boot. "Can we switch sides?"

Instead of questioning the request, he stands and waits for me to scoot over before sitting on my left side. After he's settled, I lean back into him and he wraps his arm around me.

This is more comfortable than earlier. He presses play, but I have a feeling neither of us are paying attention to the images flashing on the screen.

My arms rests on his lap, and my sweater pulls up where his hand is settled. He traces circles against my skin and another shiver courses through my body.

Sliding closer to him, I sit up and try to kiss him. My lips land on his cheek. But he doesn't say anything about the miss. He cups his free hand under my chin and closes the small gap between us. I only have a moment to freak out about the fact my breath probably tastes like popcorn and chocolate before his tongue glides along my lips.

This isn't something I usually do. I'm never this bold. But Lisa told me to take every opportunity with an open mind, and I'm doing it. Our tongues dance, and he pulls me closer to him. Careful to make sure he isn't causing me pain.

If either of us were cold before, we aren't now. It's almost too hot. Kissing him is everything I imagined it would be and more. He's not close enough. I move to straddle his lap, but my ankle hits the edge of the table, and I gasp in pain.

He pulls away, and I miss the contact. "Are you okay?"

"I think so?" The swelling has gone down, but I guess whatever muscles are in there aren't quite healed enough.

He moves me until I'm beside him and stands. Rejection courses through me. He's going to leave. We were into each other, and I ruined it. "Do you have a TV in your room?"

"Yeah, why?"

No answer. Instead, he grabs the remote, and turns off the screen in here. When he bends down, I assume he's going to tell me goodnight and leave. But he doesn't. He holds me the way he did that first night when I almost fell with the crutches.

Wrapping my arms around his neck, I let him carry me to my bedroom. The only thoughts coursing through my head are if I put away my laundry and cleaned up this morning.

He sets me on the bed before walking out. Maybe he is leaving.

Not even a minute later he comes back with the few throw pillows I have, and puts them under my injured foot. What on earth is his plan here?

"May I?" He points to the bed.

He keeps surprising me, but I can't force words out of my mouth so I nod. He climbs onto the bed next to me and grabs the blanket at the bottom, pulling it up to cover us. "I'll start the movie over."

It may seem dumb, but the background noise helps drown out the thoughts running rampant in my head. Allows me to be truly in the moment, wherever that may lead.

17

bryce

I MUST HAVE REALLY PROVED myself tonight. Not that I'm complaining. This is what I was hoping for when she caught my attention. But after the brief pause when she was in pain, I don't know what to do. "Do you, um, want to continue where we left off?"

Her mouth on mine is all the response I need. I'm careful as I pull her toward me, not wanting a repeat of what happened in the living room. She manages to pull the pillows propping her foot up with her, and I don't know how she did it, but I also don't really care. All that matters is her in my arms, and making sure she feels anything but pain.

Her hand lifts the bottom of my shirt, sliding under, and gliding over every inch of skin she can touch. I shiver at the coolness, and she yanks her hand back. Pulling away she whispers, "Sorry."

"You're fine," I kiss along her jaw, "the coldness of your hands took me by surprise."

She rubs them against her pants and touches my waist. "Better?"

"Mhhm." My lips meet hers once again, and I move until I'm hovering over her. Giving me better access to all of her.

My lips move from her mouth to her jaw, and down her neck until I meet the fabric of her shirt, she doesn't waste time in taking it off and throwing it somewhere to the side. She leaves her bra on, and I wonder if it's because removing it will cause more vulnerability than she's ready to give. "Keep going."

I do as I'm told. My lips trailing down her body. Her comfort is what's most important to me, though. "Is this okay?"

"Yeah." It's breathy when it leaves her mouth.

"Let me know if you want to stop." She reaches for my shirt and pulls at it. I sit up and yank it over my head before tossing it in the direction of her shirt. Her eyes move from my face down my chest, falling at the top of my pants, indecision passing through them. "It's okay if you don't want to go any further."

I know without a doubt we're both into each other, but I also know it's our first date. And, she's not the type of person who sleeps with someone unless her heart is one hundred percent on board. It's not something I can fault her for either. Especially when it comes to me. I unknowingly made her feel like crap all those years ago, and I don't want to do that again.

"Are you sure?" She moves her arms until they are covering her chest.

Smiling, I climb off the bed and pick our shirts up from the floor. "Absolutely."

She takes her shirt from me and rushes to put it on. "I'm so sorry. I feel like an idiot."

"Don't," I finish pulling my shirt on, "it's fine, I promise."

I go to the other side of the bed and climb in next to her. "We can finish watching this movie, then I'll go home."

There's absolutely no anger, or resentment. Maybe a little frustration, but I'll live. She stuck to what is comfortable for her, and I respect that.

"As long as you're sure." She plays with the bottom edge of her shirt.

"Don't even worry about it." I get closer to her, and put my arm around her. She seems comfortable with cuddling and I'm okay with that. At least she didn't have a problem with it earlier. Here in her bed...might be another story.

She grabs the remote and starts the movie over before shimmying closer to me. "Should we have grabbed the popcorn?"

"No, I'm fine." The beginning credits of the movie start rolling. "Unless you want it. I'll get it for you."

"It's okay. It'd probably be hard to eat while laying down."

As the movie plays, her body relaxes and the tension releases from her body. I'd like to go further with her, but not until she's ready. Not until I know without a doubt that she puts her trust in me not to hurt her.

* * *

"Wake up." There's a whisper in my ear. Someone is shaking my arm. "Bryce, wake up."

Rolling over I reach for a blanket to block out the sunlight. But there's nothing there. What the hell? This is definitely not my bed. For one, sunlight never comes through my window thanks to my blackout curtains. And my bed isn't this big.

"Bryce." My body is being moved back and forth with a lot of force. It feels like the way my brother would wake me up to get ready for school.

I bolt upright and almost hit Delilah in the face. "Oh my God. Are you okay?"

She nods and scoots back. "I didn't mean to freak you out. We both fell asleep last night, and I figured you might want to go home and get ready. Or, um, do whatever you need to do before we have to go back in later this afternoon."

"Me falling asleep at your house is becoming a habit."

"You're not wrong." She nods and slides out of bed. "I'll be right back." She hops on one foot toward her bedroom door.

"What are you doing?"

She stops and leans against the wall. "I need to grab my boot."

Why is this woman so freaking stubborn? She could have asked me. I slide out of bed and rush to her side. Before she has a chance to say anything, I scoop her off her feet and set her on the bed. "Wait here."

In less than two minutes, I'm back with her boot in hand. She crosses her arms over her chest as I slip it onto her foot and tighten the straps. "I'm perfectly capable of getting it."

"I know. But there's no need to put stress on your foot if I'm here to grab it for you." Taking a step back, I put my hand out to help her off the bed, despite just getting griped out about her being able to do things on her own. She takes it and allows me to help her.

"Thank you."

"You're welcome. Do you need anything before I go?"

"I don't think so. But could you pick me up earlier than normal? There's something I want to show you."

That's cryptic. "Any hints on what it is?"

She shakes her head and walks toward the front of the house. "Nope. You'll just have to trust me."

Surprises have never been my thing. Not because I don't like the, but I always figure out what it is before it actually happens. It pissed my sister off to no end when she tried to throw a party for my birthday one year. "Okay." Maybe I'll figure it out, maybe I won't. But I'm curious what it is she wants to show me.

The front door looms in front of us and neither of us are sure what to do now that we've crossed the line from sort of friends, to friends, and now a date. Finally, she makes the first move and wraps her arms around me for a hug. I kiss her quickly on the cheek and step away. "I'll be back in a couple of hours. Is that too early?"

"Nope. It's perfect." A ghost of smile flashes across her face. "I'll see you then."

This is the first time I've ever dated a girl at a slow pace. She needs to trust me, though, and I'll do whatever I can to earn it. To show her I'm not the guy I was in high school. If it means moving at a snail's pace, so be it.

18

delilah

"WHAT ARE WE DOING HERE?" The local recreation center is in front of us. He parked close to the entrance so the walk isn't as long for me. For a second, I think I've made a mistake bringing him here, but it's only confusion in his voice.

"I want to show you something." Without waiting for a response, I open the car door and get out. His car door closes before I have a chance to close mine. "It'll be worth it." At least, I hope it will.

He slows his pace to match mine in case I need help as we make our way toward the doors. I'm not usually one to accept help. Probably because I've always been overshadowed by my brother's accomplishments. I don't resent my twin, but it's nice to have the focus on me for once. Especially from a guy I never thought would see me. I mean he didn't back then, but he does now. Every moment we spend together makes me fall for him harder than I thought possible. Right now, my only hope is it won't crash and burn in my face. I'm not sure I could handle that while he's also working with me.

The door opens as someone is leaving and we hurry through while they hold it open. Well, I go as fast as I can. The crutches made me unbearably slow, but the boot is awkward and I can't walk as fast as I normally would. "Thank you." Both of us call out at the same time.

"Okay, so what is it you want me to see?" He looks around the building that no doubt houses many memories from his childhood. This is where all the young athletes came to play ball. It's also where a lot of them worked out during off season or when the weight room at the school was closed.

Bouncing balls come from a room ahead of us and I shuffle toward it. I'll be so happy when this boot is gone. It's really annoying, though it makes me realize how hard it must be for people living with disabilities every day. Maybe when all this is said and done, I'll find a way to help those that need it. Even if it's a small task.

We come to the door of the gym. There are two courts side by side. Each filled with young players going through basketball drills. "This."

He scrunches his eyebrows, clearly confused. It's actually adorable. "I don't play basketball."

Rolling my eyes, I pull him further into the gym. "I know that. But, look at the guys coaching them."

His eyes move around the gym, falling on two of the coaches. One is on the younger side, probably fresh out of high school and looking for something to fill his time while he's home for break. The other man is older. I'm pretty sure he used to coach at one of the schools, but keeping up with sports was never my thing.

From the way Bryce's eyes widen, I know he recognizes him. "Why would he coach little league sports when he could have a job at any high school he wants?"

"You'd have to ask him," I motion my hand toward the court, "but I'm guessing he finds joy in coaching the next generation of basketball players."

He glances around the gym and finds what he's looking for. He grabs a chair and pulls it to a wall as far away from the court as possible. "Do you mind if I talk to him?"

"Not at all." I take a seat in the chair he got for me, and watch as he jogs across the court.

Hopefully this does what I intend. He can see that he has options when it comes to fulfilling his dream of coaching. It doesn't have to be at the school level. He can start when they are young.

He shakes the coach's hand before pulling him aside. Bryce crosses his arms over his chest and nods along to whatever the coach is telling him. I wish I was close enough to hear. Close enough to see if my idea of showing him other options is working. But no, all I get are nods and random hand movements.

The suspense is killing me. Maybe it's also for selfish reasons. If he doesn't have to go back for a teaching certificate he won't leave. If he's for sure staying, it means I get more time with him. Maybe that's pathetic on my part, but the more time I've spent with him, the more my feelings come back. He has managed to get under my skin, and now I don't want him to leave.

A few minutes later, he jogs back to me. Without hesitation he lifts me off the chair and spins me around. "Thank you for bringing me here."

A giggle escapes me before he sets me down next to him. "You're welcome."

"How did you know?"

"Know what?" I grab his hand and lead him toward the hallway.

His thumb runs along the back of my hand as he gathers

his thoughts. "That I needed to talk to someone outside of the school system. To see what was possible."

"What all did he say?" We're at the doors to go out, but he pulls me to the side.

A smile graces his lips and he looks happy. I mean, I've seen him happy when we're hanging out, but this is different. It's his passion. "He saw the way my nephew played after I coached him during football season."

"I didn't know you coached the team."

"I didn't. I only helped David," he pauses for a second, "he wanted to be the star quarterback and I came home on the weekends to help him. Honestly, I don't think there's anything I wouldn't do to help that kid."

He's nothing like he was in high school. That guy didn't seem to care about anything other than the next game, or party. Unless I misjudged him even then. I don't really know what he was like because I didn't get the chance. "That's very sweet of you."

"Yeah, well, he's my nephew," he shrugs and pushes the door open, "but Coach Powers told me they are always looking for people to help out around here with the youth in the community. Sports gives them something to do and keeps them out of trouble. I should know."

"Will your degree work with that?"

He leads me to the car and walks me to the passenger side door. "I don't even really need my degree, but he also said I could offer private lessons and be at games in case of emergencies."

"Is that something you might want to do?" Please say yes.

"Actually, yeah." Opening the door, he waits until I get in to shut it. He jogs in front and gets behind the wheel. "It's not coaching at the schools. But it'll give me a chance to see if that's something I really want to do. Then I can decide whether or not I want to get the teaching certificate."

"That sounds like a solid plan."

He starts the car before grabbing my hand . "It does. For once it seems like things are going my way."

Let's hope they continue that way. The nervousness I felt about bringing him here is long gone. He gets the best of both worlds. Doing what he loves and sticking around to make an impact in the community he grew up in.

"I'm glad."

"It's all thanks to you." He kisses my hand and backs out of the parking spot.

He's put all of his trust in me, and I'm still scared to completely open up to him. That's something I need to change.

19

bryce

"MOM," my voice is muffled by the coats in the closet as I rummage through boxes, "do you have any extra tree decorations?"

Her footsteps are loud as she comes down the hallway from her room. "What?"

I pop my head out of the closet. "Do you have any extra tree decorations?"

"Yes. But why are you looking in the closet?"

Glancing between her and the closet, I shrug my shoulders. "That's where they were not too long ago. Where else would they be?"

"In the shed out back." She opens the door wider to see what mess I've made. "I only kept them in here until I had a chance to take them out there."

"Oh." Bending over, I put the boxes back in place and do my best to make it look the way it was. "Do you mind if I borrow some of them?"

"For what?"

"Delilah doesn't have a tree in her place, so I bought her one. But I didn't think about the ornaments until now."

A sly grin replaces her confused frown. "Sure. There are a few packages of matching ornaments in one of the boxes. I can pull them out for you in a bit."

"I'll look for them." I grab a jacket out of the closet before closing the door. "I'm supposed to be over there in less than an hour with lunch."

She opens her mouth, but doesn't have a chance to say anything. I'm already rushing through the kitchen to the back door. Cold air hits me in the face as soon as I open it. Winter has barely started here, and I'm already over it.

The shed door creaks as I open it. The room is dark, even with the faint sunlight coming through the small windows. I grab my phone and turn on the flashlight.

There are two boxes up front label Christmas. I pull the lid off both boxes, and shine the light inside one then the other. The second one has two boxes of bold, jewel-colored ornaments. I'm certain these were the ones mom was talking about.

Scooping both packages of ornaments out of the box, I set them on the ground before putting the lid back. I pick up the lid of the other box and lower it until something catches my eye.

Mistletoe. At least, that's what I think it is. It looks like the decoration Delilah hung in all the entryways of the bar. Screw it, I pick it up and add it to the stack of ornaments before putting the lid back on the box.

It feels like the temperature has dropped even more the few minutes I was in the shed. With the chances of rain up, there's a good chance we'll get flurries at some point today. Maybe even tonight.

I trudge back inside and close the door behind me. "I found them, Mom."

She's standing by the coffee pot waiting for it to fill her cup. "Good. Are you leaving?"

Nodding I head toward the front door. "I just have to grab my keys and wallet."

"Okay. Be careful out there. If the weather gets bad, stay put."

"Yes, Mom." I roll my eyes. Finding an apartment is being moved up my list. I love her with all my heart, but she can be a tad overprotective.

"I'm serious, Bryce." Turning I face her. "I'd rather know you're safe than wonder if you've slid into a ditch."

"Okay. I'll keep you updated. At least I don't have to work tonight."

"Thank goodness for small favors."

She worries about me and it's adorable. I walk back toward her and give her a hug. "You be careful, too, if you go out."

"I'm not getting out of my jammies." She grins. "Love you."

She shoos me away and I take it as my cue to leave. "Love you, too," I call over my shoulder.

Now to pick up lunch and surprise Delilah. Hopefully this isn't overstepping, but I won't know until she sees everything.

* * *

The front door opens before I even knock. Which is a good thing because I'm close to dropping everything in my arms. Hopefully she wasn't watching me struggle getting all this to the porch without making two trips.

"What's all this?" She eyes the box by my feet and the ones in my arms.

"Surprise." I want to do jazz hands that go with the word,

but I'll break everything. "I, uh, noticed you didn't have a tree and figured I'd bring some holiday joy inside."

She doesn't say anything and I'm worried I've mis-stepped. "Let me help you." She grabs the bag of food out of one hand and one of the boxes out from under my arm.

"Thanks." I step inside long enough to set the other box down and then turn to pick up the tree. Rain drops hit the box and I'm happy that waited until I got here. It's a good thing I put an extra set of clothes in the back seat in case I don't go home tonight. Lessons learned from the last time I fell asleep here.

"You didn't have to do this," she tries to hide the small smile on her lips, "but thank you."

"You're welcome." I set the tree down beside the coffee table. "Is in front of the window a good spot for it?"

"Sure." She grabs the remote and plays a random Christmas movie while I pull the tree out of the box. "I guess today is kind of the perfect day to do it with the weather."

"It really is. Especially if it snows later."

"What? I didn't know it was going to do that." She looks at the rain coming down. "You're more than welcome to stay here if the roads get bad."

"Thanks." I stack the pieces on top of each other until the tree is complete. Next step, fluffing. I pull the branches apart and move them around until it looks full.

I'm surprised Delilah hasn't come to help, but when I turn around, she has the food set out on the coffee table and a can of coke beside each plate.

"It looks good," she motions toward the couch. "Come eat. We can decorate it in a bit."

Both of us eat the food pretty quickly and she moves the plates to the kitchen while I plug in the lights. They really brighten up the small space.

I grab the box of ornaments, pull one out, and hand it to her.

"What are you doing?" She takes it and holds it in front of her, watching the lights from the tree twinkle in the reflection.

"It's only right that you hang up the first one."

"Oh." She walks around the tree, looking for the perfect spot. Finally, she finds one about halfway up in the front. "There."

We both take turns placing the ornaments on the tree, doing our best to make sure they aren't clustered together. It's something I learned to make an effort with because my mom would get so annoyed when they were all in one spot.

The now empty boxes are on the floor and I pick them and put them inside the tree box. "I'm going to set these over here. You'll need it when the tree goes down."

"Who knows, maybe I'll keep it up year-round."

"Like those seasonal trees people post on social media."

"Yep." She takes a step back and takes in our handy work. "It's perfect. Thank you so much."

I dig around in my jacket pocket and pull out the last piece. Reaching up, I put the mistletoe as high on the tree as I can. "Now it's finished."

"Is that what I think it is?" She takes a step forward and stands on her toes to inspect it.

"Yep." My steps are slow and measured as I close the distance between us.

20

delilah

BRYCE TOWERS OVER ME. The mistletoe directly above us and I don't make him wait a second longer than it took him to come closer to me.

I lean up as far as I can and lift up my foot with boot. My arms go around his neck and my lips meet his. This time, I'm not going to pull away. I'm not going to step on the breaks.

He lifts me up, and my legs wrap around his waist. His hands cradle my ass to keep me secure, and I suck in a breath at the touch. Never in my life have I had someone hold me like this.

Breaking the kiss, he pulls back, leaving a couple of inches between his mouth and mine. "Is this okay?"

"Yes." The word is a whisper on my lips. An invitation for him to continue.

"Are you sure? I don't want you to do anything you're not ready for."

I love the fact he's a gentleman, but that's not what I want right now. He's gone above and beyond anything I could have imagined. From stopping the other night when I had a moment of uncertainty, to buying me a freaking tree. Every car ride, and night of movies makes me fall head over heels for him all over again.

Unhooking my legs, I slide down his body until my feet meet the ground. I don't miss the bulge in his pants, and I don't want to be his cause for frustration twice.

I grab his hand and lead him to my room. If he won't believe my words, then I'll have to show him with actions. When it's just us and I don't get lost in my own thoughts, he boosts my confidence far higher than I ever could on my own.

He brings us to a stop at the bedroom door. "Delilah, we don't have to do anything." He must see the pang of rejection I feel because he continues. "Not that I don't want you. I do, more than you know. But only if you're ready. I don't want to pressure you into anything."

This is something I've thought about for years. I shoved it out of my head thinking it wasn't a possibility. But it's a reality. He's here. Now. In my room. And I'm damn sure not being pressured.

"Bryce, if you want me, you'll do something about it."

That's all the permission he needs. He scoops me up and places me on the bed. His mouth melts into mine and his hand traces the outline of my body. Fingers grazing my breast before tracing down my side, and finally toying with the edge of my leggings.

The simple touch causes heat to rush south, and I start pushing down my pants. He pulls away and kisses a trail down my chest, stomach, and backs up until he's standing over me. Want fills his dark brown eyes, and he gets on his knees at the edge of the bed.

He takes his time loosening the straps on my boot before pulling it off. He grabs the waistband of my pants, and panties, and they join my boot on the floor. It's hot and I yank my shirt over my head, tossing it somewhere behind me.

Before I can demand he kiss me again, he grabs my thighs and pulls my body to the edge of the bed. He turns his head and kisses my calf before looking up at me. "Are you still okay?"

I nod. It's all I can do. Words don't form because it's happening. Not that I'm a virgin or anything, but this is special for me. Probably more than he realizes.

His lips move along my skin, going further up with each one until he's reached his goal. My legs are hooked over his shoulders, but he keeps one hand on my right leg to keep my ankle elevated. Always thinking of ways to make sure I don't get hurt.

His tongue circles my clit and I lean my head back, relishing the feel of his mouth on me. Seconds later his finger slides into me and pumps three times before he crooks his finger, reaching the spot most men miss. Oh. My. God. I see stars as I come apart.

It's almost embarrassing how quickly I come, but the anticipation of being with Bryce and the way his tongue works magic...it was bound to happen.

He moves until he's hovering over me. My hands go straight to his pants and I undo the button, frantically pushing them down.

His chuckle is deeper than normal, and I know he's as turned on as I am. I've thought about what could have happened the other night more than I'd like to admit. "Shit. I don't have a condom."

"Top drawer of the dresser."

"You were prepared for this to happen?" Leaning over he opens the drawer and pulls a one out. "I'm beginning to think you planned on taking advantage of me today."

"I was open to the possibility."

He kicks his pants off the rest of the way and rolls the condom over his cock. I've never actually seen the person I'm with put one on. It's usually dark in the room.

"Good to know." He wraps one arm under my waist and pushes me toward the middle of the bed. "Is your ankle okay?"

"Not even a concern right now." I pull him down until his lips meet mine. I can taste myself and that's another new experience for me. It's not bad, just different.

Widening my legs, he settles between them before slowly pressing into me. It's sweet the care he takes. I'm not sure if he thinks I've never had sex, but I like that he cares enough to take his time.

I hook my arms under his, bringing him closer to me. Feeling his skin against mine takes the intimacy up a thousand notches. His thrusts come faster and harder, the rhythm picking up in time with our breathing.

He breaks the kiss leans his forehead against the bed next to me. I'm close, and I have a feeling he is too. I wrap my uninjured leg over his waist, pulling him deeper into me. That's all it takes for him to come undone. I follow after. Our breathing loud enough to be heard throughout the house. I've never been more grateful to not have a roommate than I am right now.

"I promise, I usually last longer." His laugh is wobbly, nervous.

"I think we both got a little too excited." I kiss his cheek and wait for him to move. Not because I want him to, but because I need to clean up.

When he does, he grabs my hand, holding it between us. "So, I guess it's a good thing we didn't have to work today."

"For sure." Even though I'm freaking out on the inside, I'm doing my best to stay calm and collected on the outside. "Want to watch a movie?"

"By the Christmas tree?" He's really proud of that thing,

but I get it. The tree brought me joy, and that's exactly what he wanted to do.

"Absolutely." I roll over and give him a quick kiss. "I'll even make hot chocolate."

"Sounds like a plan." He helps me stand and grabs my clothes from the floor. It takes him a few moments to find my shirt, but soon enough he's helping me to the restroom. "I'll pick out a movie."

I've barely gotten my clothes on when he calls my name from the living room. "Del, come look."

Quickly, I shove my shirt over my head, and put the boot on my foot. The straps are barely tight enough to keep the boot from coming off.

I come to a halt when I get to the living room and see what he's looking at.

His gaze is focused on the window, and the small white flurries coming down outside. "I guess that means you're staying the night."

"It looks that way."

"Good."

"You sit down, I'll make the hot chocolate." I watch him walk toward the kitchen. The cabinets open and the mugs hit the counter with a thud. I couldn't think of a more perfect way to spend the evening with the man I'm falling for all over again.

21

bryce

BEING home feels a lot better now that I have a plan in place. A way to use part of my degree and follow my passion. Plus-side, I'll be instilling routines these kids can take with them into their high school and college playing. It helps that I get to spend it with the girl I'm falling for, even though it feels like it's going too fast.

"You're going to be late," Mom calls from somewhere at the front of the house.

She's not wrong. We have the opening of the stage area tonight. Instead of opening for lunch, Angie closed down until it's closer to evening. Which was fine by me. I got to sleep in this morning and it felt nice.

Even though I'm working, I check my clothes one more time. Black shirt and jeans. Simple and classic. Stella and Angie wanted us to look uniform, and this was the only thing all of us could agree on. Eric was trying to talk her into ugly sweaters, and Angie nixed that pretty quickly.

Grabbing my phone and wallet, I head out of my room.

Mom is on the couch with a mug in her hand. I'm not sure if it's coffee or hot chocolate, but there's no telling. "I'll be back at some point. I'm not sure what cleanup is going to look like yet."

"It's fine dear," she waves me off, "if you end up staying at Delilah's again, just let me know. And make sure you're using protection."

"Mom," I shriek. At this point I shouldn't be surprised by what comes out of her mouth. But I guess that's what happens after three kids. You just say whatever pops out of your mouth.

"Fine, I'll leave you alone about Delilah." She takes a sip out of her mug before mumbling something about how cute we are together.

"Bye, Mom." If I don't get out of here soon, she'll be planning our wedding next. We've barely even started dating. I definitely don't need her freaking either one of us out with talk of things that may, or may not, happen in the future.

As soon as I'm in the car, I turn the heat on high to warm the car up before I get to Delilah's house. Hopefully she's ready because we'll be cutting it close getting to work as it is.

Looking both ways I back out of the driveway. After a couple of turns, I'm at Delilah's. There was no need worrying about her being ready. She's already on the porch, locking the door before I've got the car parked.

"Wow, you're running late today," she says as she slides into the car. She's getting faster with the boot, and almost back to her normal speed. Though I wish she would have let me get the door for her.

"Sorry," I mutter, "Mom was being weird."

"How so?"

"You really don't want to know." She might, though. I'm too embarrassed to tell her, and I don't want to bring it up. "Are you ready for tonight?"

When in doubt, change the subject. It seems to work most of the time. She lays her hand on top of mine, and stares out the window.

"I'm not sure," she sighs, "it will be great for the bar, don't get me wrong, but I worry about the trouble it might bring."

Yeah, I feel her on that, especially after the run-in with the guy who was being a dick to her the night she helped me. "We can cross our fingers nothing happens."

"I'm sure everything will be fine. Angie won't let things get out of hand."

She's still worried despite how much she's trying to reassure herself. Not that I blame her. This is a pretty big change for the bar, and she can't get around the way she normally would if things should go awry.

"It's going to be great. And...there won't be as many issues with people having to wait outside until more room is opened up."

"You're right," she nods. "Everything is going to be great. The decorations will be talked about, and people are going to love the person we have opening."

Huh, I never thought to ask who would be performing tonight. My mouth moves to ask, but it's something I should probably already know and decide to let it be a surprise.

It's almost closing time. People are starting to leave the dance floor and pay their tabs. Even more surprising is the fact Delilah's brother, Devin, is the performer tonight. I always thought music was something he fooled around with, but it looks like I didn't know him as well as I thought I did. I'm glad he's following his passion.

With the crowd dwindling, I take the moment to woo Delilah. She's sitting at the podium with her chair turned toward the stage on the other side of the bar. I know she's not much of a people person, but I can tell she would rather be moving around instead of sitting up front watching everyone.

Now's my chance. I wrap my arms around her waist before sliding her off the stool. "What are you doing?"

With one hand, I move her arms around my neck. "Dancing with you, silly."

Luckily, it's a slow song and doesn't require a lot of movement. She steps on my foot with her boot, and I do my best to hide my wince.

She tries to pull away, but I keep her close. Her stepping on my foot isn't enough for me to let her go. Over her head, Eric gives me a thumbs up, as if he had anything to do with this spur of the moment decision.

The song ends and she takes a step back. "Thank you."

"No, thank you." I bend down and give her a quick peck on the cheek. "I need to make sure everyone over there makes their way out and start cleaning up. You good here?"

"Yeah, I'm good." Her smile is brighter than every light strand in this bar, and I'm the one who put it there.

Luckily everyone here is local and knows Angie's a stickler about them leaving at closing time. We don't have to force anyone out.

I begin cleaning up while Devin and his band break down their set. It looks like the grand opening of the dance floor and stage area were a huge success. Thank God it's only on Friday and Saturday nights. I don't know that any of us could handle the amount of clean up if it was every night.

It doesn't take us long to get all the glasses to the kitchen. Even the bartenders are helping clean up in here. They usually only do the bar area. All that's left is mopping and wiping down the tables.

Delilah grabs a rag and begins that process while I get the

mop and bucket. Each person is covering a section. At this rate, we may all get home before one.

The bell above the door tinkles. it must be Devin and the band heading out. The mop is yanked out of my hands, and I turn around ready to argue with whoever is making my job difficult.

Devin laughs and gives me a quick hug. "Hey, man. It's been a while."

"Yeah, it has. How've you been?"

"Pretty good," he hands me the mop and I continue the task at hand, "singing now."

"I heard. You're not so bad."

"Shut up," he lightly punches me in the arm. "So, you and my sister, huh?"

I sneak a glance in her direction. "Yeah, it's pretty new." She's standing at the podium looking in our direction. The chairs in the seated area are already up on the tables. This is the only place left to clean.

"You know she had a crush on you all throughout high school, right?"

"Yeah, I know that now."

He looks around the empty space. "Any chance they'd let us get a beer and catch up?"

"Probably not," I shake my head, "but you can come over any time I'm not working."

"Bryce," Carlos yells my name. "Speed it up. The rest of us are ready to go."

"Almost done." I finish up the last of the room and set the mop back into the bucket. "I've gotta get your sister home. I'll see you later."

"If you'll be up for a bit, I can be at your house in twenty."

Shit. I didn't realize he meant tonight. Delilah is still watching us and nods toward the door. "Um, let me check with Delilah. You still have the same number?" He nods. "I'll let you know."

After he heads out, I take care of the mop water and get the supplies put away. Delilah is standing by the front door. "Are you finally ready?"

Her smile is tight and I can't help but wonder what that's about. "Yeah, let's get out of here."

I'm not sure what has upset her, but I aim to find out.

22

delilah

THE RIDE to my house is silent aside from Christmas music playing on the radio. I'm still shocked he loves the holidays as much as he does.

"So, the opening went well." Small talk...that's what we've resorted to.

"Yeah, it did," my gaze stays at the window. "Guess I didn't have anything to worry about."

"Nope," I can hear the smile in his voice. "That might change for New Year's Eve, though. Carlos mentioned we'd be having a pretty big name playing."

"Yep. It's that band Crooked Halo."

"No shit?" Out of the corner of my eye, I can see him shaking his head. "How did Angie and Stella manage that?"

"Stella's cousin's fiancé manages their website and merchandise." It's a pretty cool gig, I have to admit. But I'm also excited to see them play. I've been a fan since I found them online.

"That's pretty awesome." He pulls into my driveway and

gets out of the car, walking over to my side of the car. The door opens and he holds his hand out.

For a split second, I debate taking it. It's dumb, I know. But he acted if as if nobody else existed the second my brother went to him. Just like old times, them in their own little world.

Placing my hand in his, I allow him to help me from the car. He walks me to the door and waits for me to unlock it. I could dawdle, but I don't. It's cold out here and I don't want to be outside longer than I have to.

"Do you want to come in?" This is the easiest way to handle the situation of whether he wants to stay with me or go hang out with my brother. Childish? Maybe. Past hurts can't be helped, though.

"Why wouldn't I?" The confusion that passes over his face is almost too much to bear. This is it. When I let him know just how insecure I am. With any luck it won't make him run for the hills.

I leave the door open so he can follow me inside if he chooses to. Before I make it to the couch, I hear the door close behind me. I'm too much of a coward to turn around. Too afraid to see if he is going to forget about me and go back to the way things used to be with my brother.

"Del." His steps are almost silent as he makes his way to me. His fingers graze the side of my arm. "What's going on? I thought things were okay with us."

How do I tell him my biggest fear without looking like a pathetic, scared little girl? Without becoming the teenage girl who let her emotions think there was a possibility with the star quarterback.

Bryce turns me around before guiding me to sit on the couch. He makes sure I'm on his right in case I want to move my leg under me but still in a position to face him head on.

"Please talk to me, Delilah. I can't fix whatever has happened between us if I don't know what I did."

Those are the words that make me spill my guts out to him. "You haven't done anything, Bryce."

"Then what's changed between when we danced and when we left the bar. Because something shifted."

One. Two. Three deep breaths. "My brother." His head snaps back, but I continue before he can say anything. "I saw both of you talking during clean up. I was afraid that the two of you would do your own thing and it'd be like I didn't exist...again."

Oh my God. It sounds absolutely ridiculous when I say it out loud. He must think I'm an idiot. Living all those years in my brother's shadow, and the person you crushed on the hardest not even realizing you exist...they were hard for me to handle as a teenager. You never realize how badly those things affect you as you get older until you're thrust in similar situations.

He doesn't say anything, and it feels like my fears are coming to fruition. I'm an idiot. I should have kept my mouth shut and acted like everything was okay. Like the possibility of me be forgotten wouldn't have completely destroyed any confidence I've built.

Any minute he's going to get up and walk out the door. And I'll be stuck here sitting beside the Christmas tree he got me being sad.

Instead, he slips his fingers through mine and places his other one on top. "That's not going to happen."

"How do I know that?"

He lifts one hand from mine and cups my cheek. The warmth sweeping through me. "You're going to have to trust me."

"I'm still scared." Another admission I didn't mean to say out loud.

"Don't be." He leans forward until his forehead is touching mine. That's definitely not something I'd expect from someone who wants to forget about me. "He asked me to hang out with him tonight."

I suck in a breath. I knew it. Before I can say anything, he continues. "Don't worry. I told him I had to check with you before letting him know. I wasn't sure if you wanted to hang out and watch movies, or if you were exhausted after tonight."

"Won't he be upset you chose me over him?"

"Who cares if he does? I'm dating *you*. Not him. And he's definitely not someone I can cuddle with while watching cheesy holiday movies."

A giggle slips through my lips. "I think I'd almost pay to see that. I'm sorry for acting weird. It's just hard to push aside that feeling of being ignored."

"Your feelings are valid, just don't push me away." He leans in for a quick kiss. "Besides, I don't think there's any way I could ever forget who you are again."

Good to know. It's still shocking that he chose me over hanging out with his friend, even if it is my brother. Especially since they haven't seen each other in a long time. But I need to know that I'm not some passing infatuation. "Why is that?"

He scoots away from me, and I immediately regret asking. Taking me by surprise, he pulls me over until I'm in his lap, my booted foot hanging awkwardly to the side.

"Because," he grins, "you don't make fun of me for my holiday cheer. You helped me find solutions to my career decision problems without giving up my passions. You make me laugh, and have a different outlook on life. And it may be way too fucking soon to say this, but I'm falling in love with you each and every time we are together."

If I was standing, this is the moment I'd swoon and fall into his arms. Luckily, I'm already in his lap. I throw my arms around his neck and smash my lips into his. This might be the best gift I could be given this year. The guy of my dreams is mine in real life. Eighteen-year old me would have never believed it.

Laughing, he pulls away after a few minutes. "I guess it's safe to say you feel the same way?"

"Was I not convincing?" I try lifting an eyebrow, but I can't and I'm sure I look ridiculous.

"You were. But you should stop doing that with your face."

Smacking him lightly on the chest, I move off his lap. "I was trying to be cute." The remote is on the table and I nod toward it. "More cheesy Christmas movies?"

"Yes. Roulette style. I'll make the popcorn and hot chocolate."

While he's doing that, I grab the remote and search the holiday movies. So much has changed since he moved back to town. Before, I was lonely, missing my friend and not feeling the holidays. Now...now I have everything I could have possibly wanted despite my fear trying to hold me back. Me and Bryce? We're going to be alright.

epilogue

NEW YEAR'S EVE. A time for new beginnings and adventures. I never thought I'd end up with the sister of one of my friend's. Hell, I didn't realize he had a sister until she pointed it out. That may have been the best night I've had in a while. Because Delilah? She's it for me. She gets me in a way not even my siblings do.

"It's almost midnight, we need to get the champagne out." The person in question comes to my side. The boot is gone, and without the soft thuds of it hitting the floor, she sneaks up on me more than I care to admit.

"You got it." We walk side by side to the bar to pick up trays of champagne filled flutes. Nobody has to watch the door because for tonight only, we sold tickets in advance for the show.

"You take this side, and I'll grab the folks in front of the stage." She nods toward where her brother's band is playing. They won't be up there for long. After midnight, Crooked Halo will be taking the stage. "Eric has some champagne set aside for the rest of us behind the bar. But you can have mine."

"Why?" I shift the tray in my hands to keep it balanced. I'm slowly learning how to hold these when they are full.

"Because I don't like champagne."

"Oh." Then she won't be getting champagne, but she'll have something to bring in the new year. "I'll meet you by the podium when we're done."

She nods and heads off to the other half of the bar while I hand a glass to everyone on this side. Once my tray is empty, I scan the area to make sure Delilah isn't anywhere to be seen, and I make my way to the bar.

Eric pulls out the tray of champagne he had set aside for us, and I shake my head. "Del doesn't like it. What does she usually get when she's not on the clock?"

He doesn't answer me, but he gets to work making two of the same drink. Various bottles are pulled from the shelf. This will be new for me. I've only stuck to beer or whiskey. Never anything with that many things in it.

Finally, he sets the two glasses in front of me. "What are they?"

"It's a mai tai," he tilts his head to the side, "have you never had one?"

"Nope," I shake my head, "why does she like these?"

"Because it reminds me of the beach." She stands next to me. "It's my go to drink when it's cold because then I can pretend I'm sitting in sand, watching the waves roll in."

"Makes since." I bring the drink to my mouth, but she bumps into me.

"Not yet. We have to wait until the countdown."

"Fine." I tap the bar and watch the clock. There are only a few minutes until it's officially a new year.

Someone pounds on the door and one of the bartenders, who never seems to work the same time I do, rushes to see what the commotion is.

After a few whispered words a blond girl runs in. Her eyes

widen as soon as she sees Delilah, and she makes a beeline for her. "Lilah, it's been forever!"

"Lisa," Delilah yells and throws her arms around the girl who has just barged in. This is the girl who lived with Del before moving away. "What are you doing here?"

"I'm back." Lisa lets go of my girlfriend and smiles. "For good this time."

"You sure about that?" Delilah teases.

"Definitely. The world out there doesn't hold the family I have here." She notices the stage and gasps, "it's finally finished. And...Devin is playing?"

"Yeah, he's opening for the next act." Delilah grins while looking at the stage. No doubt proud of him for going after what he wants. "How did you get in?"

"I bought a ticket. I had no idea it was going to be a concert. I thought it was just a party." When Del turns back toward the bar, I don't miss the way her friend's eyes linger on the man on the stage. There's no way in hell Delilah would be okay with her looking at her brother that way, but I'm not going to say anything.

"Lucky you." She grabs one of the flutes of champagne and hands it to Lisa. "We're about to do the midnight toast."

Lisa looks between the both of us and smirks. "I'll just go over there." She winks before joining the crowd.

The music stops and Devin starts the countdown at one minute before midnight. Everyone chants along with him. I put my arm around Delilah and bring her in closer.

Five. Four. Three. Two. One. "Happy New Year" is yelled throughout the room, and people are toasting. Our drinks are forgotten as I take that moment to pull my girlfriend into a kiss. The only way to start the new year off right.

I have a new job, new friends, and the best girl. I couldn't ask for anything more. Who knows, maybe this summer we'll actually enjoy those drinks on the beach.

acknowledgments

Thank you so much to my family for giving me the space and time I needed to write this book. Also, for keeping me on track when it came to sitting down to write it.

My first grandchild was also born while writing this so I want to give a quick thank you to my son and his girlfriend for giving the family such a cute little human to cuddle.

My friends, team, and everyone else involved, I couldn't do this without you. Thank you for constantly being my support system. Y'all rock!

And you, reader, thank you for picking up each new book. For always taking a chance on me and my characters. I hope you are excited for more stories from the Out of the Ashes crew.

also by katrina marie

Out of the Ashes

Cocktails & Crushes

Brews & Bartenders

Mai Tais & Mistletoe

Martinis & Musicians

The Taking Chances Series

Welcome to Your Life

Cruel and Beautiful World

Ways to Go

Remember That Night

My Only Wish is You

From This Moment

Shoot Down the Stars

Love Will Save Your Soul

Cousins Gone RomCom Series

Gone Country

Gone Steady

Gone Again

Cocky Hero Club

Big Baller

Silverwood Bulldog Series

Baseball & Broadway

about the author

Katrina Marie lives in the Dallas area with her husband, two children, bonus child, grandchild, and two fur babies. She is a lover of all things geeky and nerdy. When she's not writing you can find her at her children's sporting events, or curled up reading a book.

You can find Katrina Marie online in the following places:
Sign up for my newsletter: https://www.subscribepage.com/KatrinaMarieNewsletter
Website: katrinamarieauthor.com

facebook.com/katrinamarieauthor

twitter.com/katmarieauthor

instagram.com/katrinamarieauthor

bookbub.com/profile/katrina-marie

pinterest.com/katrinamarieauthor

tiktok.com/@katrinamarieauthor

patreon.com/katrinamarie